74110   595

FIC
FRI

Fry, Alan

The revenge of
Annie Charlie

DATE DUE			
NOV 3- '75			
MAY 20 '77			
FAC '89			

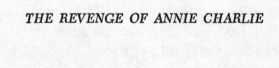

THE REVENGE OF ANNIE CHARLIE

Books by Alan Fry
THE REVENGE OF ANNIE CHARLIE
COME A LONG JOURNEY
HOW A PEOPLE DIE
RANCH ON THE CARIBOO

ALAN FRY

The Revenge
of Annie Charlie

74110

DOUBLEDAY CANADA LIMITED, TORONTO, ONTARIO
DOUBLEDAY & COMPANY, INC., GARDEN CITY, NEW YORK
1973

ISBN: 0-385-06257-5
Library of Congress Catalog Card Number 73–79666
Copyright © 1973 by Alan Fry
Printed in the United States of America
First Edition

TO MY MARGERY

THE REVENGE OF ANNIE CHARLIE

I

Two or three times or more a week Big Meadow Charlie
would make his way in his shuffling limp out to his ancient
horse barn and put the saddle on his ancient horse, then somehow pull his ponderous body into that saddle and ride the
three quarters of a mile from the Big Meadow Reserve to
Gyp's cabin at Upper Meadow. Most times it would have no
more result than that he and Gyp wouldn't say a solitary thing
to each other for anything up to four or five hours at a stretch.

Gyp had an old easy chair that he never himself used any
more, not even at night when he was tired and the chances of
Big Meadow coming on that long ride were almost negligible.
It had become by usage Big Meadow's chair and therefore not
Gyp's any longer, and as though to assure the continuance of
Big Meadow's intermittent but valued presence in his cabin,
Gyp made out between the split pine bench at the table
where he ate, and the pole bed with a hay and gunny sack
mattress where he slept.

Often Big Meadow would come there and sit for a long
time while Gyp was out doing things essential to the hay and
the cattle and the rundown horse-drawn machinery with which
he made the sketchy living that was enough for his limited
ambition. Then when Gyp returned Big Meadow would be
there, several hours of saying nothing already accomplished,
and if it was time to boil coffee or heat grub, Gyp would do
just that, as he would if the old man weren't there, except

that he'd make enough for two and they'd share it in the continuing silence.

Then something as unspoken as what had brought him in the first place would move Big Meadow Charlie to leave, and he would make his way to where he'd left his horse eating hay in Gyp's corral, and from there he'd ride home.

Then at other times he'd have a more specific purpose for his visit. After he'd let a long time go by he'd ask Gyp if he'd got a singletree or a hacksaw or a rasp or a few horseshoe nails.

And Gyp would say yeh, he thought maybe he had, and when it was time for Big Meadow to go, perhaps another hour or two later, they'd go together and find whatever it was the old man needed.

Then as a result of that there'd be visits that had the purpose of bringing something back when it was done with.

And there were visits, too, because the time was right to shoot fat buck deer on the big fir ridges to the west, or to pursue just once more the illusion they shared that somewhere on Snyder Creek there were gold nuggets to be had by the handful, if you could only find them.

And whether or not they embarked on these trips did not matter, and more often than not they didn't, for traveling had grown increasingly difficult for Big Meadow these past three years, especially with the pain in his ankle where it had been broken on the last wagon journey he had made with his family.

It was enough that the time was right for the kind of journey that they had once made together, and an afternoon could be spent quietly, each man lost in his own remembering, sharing again the companionship that those trips had been all about.

But just once in a long while Big Meadow Charlie would come to Gyp Sandhouse's cabin because there was actually something he had to say to him, and Gyp could usually tell these times because there would be a lot of false starts, a lot of ten- and twelve-word utterances of an inconsequential kind through the first long time of sitting.

"That bay stud sure makin' good horse."

To which Gyp would grunt his assent and nothing more, because for at least the past two years he and Big Meadow had been agreed on the point; ever since, in fact, Gyp had found that castrating that particular colt had been a violation of nature beyond even his almost limitless practicality.

What in God's world he would ever do on his two-dollar ranch with a stud he could not imagine, and he had taken the sex away from more calves and colts than he could begin to remember, but he had not been able to cut into that one particular little horse. There had been something in the way the colt had moved so fast by his mother, with his head held high and his neck bowed—but Gyp didn't care to think about it.

Whenever he caught himself doing things that didn't, finally, make any sense, he much preferred not to think on them further, and so he never asked himself why he didn't castrate that horse. And one of the things he liked about Big Meadow Charlie was that he never asked him either.

He'd just observe every so often: "That bay stud sure makin' good horse."

And when he'd sit in his chair in Gyp's cabin and make those kinds of observations about Gyp's horses, the state of the haying, the weather, or how his old woman was wishing he could load up a wagon and take her and all the grandchildren blueberry picking, Gyp knew that he had something important to say, and if they both waited long enough it was bound to come out.

Like the one time he had talked about Annie.

That time he hadn't started until the day had worn so late that Gyp had heaved aside the big grizzly hide that hid the trap door to the root cellar under his cabin floor and gone down into the darkness below with a lantern to fetch the onions and turnips and carrots and potatoes he needed to put with the chunk of deer meat that was simmering in a pot on the big stove in the corner of the cabin.

When he'd emerged again, Big Meadow had begun, and by the time the potatoes were cooked he'd managed to say most of what he was going to say; and that time it sounded very largely as though his old woman had put him up to it.

The guts of it had been the very simple and perfectly understandable question under the circumstances: Why didn't Gyp let Annie live with him and have kids? But it had taken the old man a long and difficult way around, in which only once did he mention Annie's name and only twice did he refer to the advantages of a good woman in a man's cabin.

Much of the rest of it had to do with what a damn lot of noise his grandchildren made and how he wished all his sons-in-law would go find shacks of their own someplace. There were three of them still at Big Meadow's cabin, and while Big Meadow's cabin was large and had an upstairs divided into sleeping rooms, his daughters were both healthy and prolific and it made for a lot of grandchildren.

And none of what Big Meadow had said that time had implied that the answer to the question was any of Big Meadow's business.

In fact, the disconnectedness of everything that the old man had said (and you were free to put it together in any order you chose), made it very clear that it was not his business and that the last thing he expected was that Gyp should make any kind of reply to it at all.

And indeed Gyp had made no response, because in truth Gyp felt just a little badly over Annie, though not badly enough to do anything more about her than he was doing already.

4

Which wasn't much at all, because if there was one thing Gyp Sandhouse aimed to avoid in life it was responsibility, and of all the kinds of responsibility he had observed in the burdens of others, the responsibility for a woman and a houseful of kids was, though it enticed you with the greatest of pleasure, perhaps altogether the most onerous.

It entailed so much and it went on for so long.

To house and feed and clothe their kids he had seen men root themselves into places they didn't like and persist year after year in jobs they didn't care for—and every time a woman had another child, her husband had renewed for himself the whole term of his servitude.

When he was a boy on his father's boulder-strewn foothills homestead, Gyp had known a man on the nearby Shumi Reserve who'd got married at nineteen, and his wife had had a child a year for most of twenty years. When this man was forty his first daughter got married and gave him a grandchild, and his wife had two more after that.

So even if he didn't end up caring for some of the grandchildren, at forty he'd been twenty-one years raising kids, and had another eighteen years of it to look forward to.

Every little while that man would get drunk and saddle his horse and roar up and down the road through the reserve. And nothing would stop him until he'd exhausted himself and his horse, and his horse would bring him home.

Gyp didn't want to invest the horseflesh and the saddle leather in the roaring up and down, much less look after the kids.

And it wasn't that he didn't like kids. He enjoyed them and they enjoyed him. Big Meadow's grandchildren crawled on his lap and spilled his tea and stuck their runny noses against his whiskered cheek, and he found it very pleasant. It was the years, not the kids, that appalled him, the endlessness of the commitment if the children happened to be yours.

5

And if you lived with the woman, the children would indeed happen to be yours. Gyp had been twenty-five when he came to Upper Meadow, and he was now thirty. But Annie was only twenty-five now, and so she could be having children when he would be forty-five, children that he could still be raising when he was sixty or more. That was the arithmetic that got to the streak in him which curled at the very thought of responsibility.

And all this was a huge disappointment to Annie. Ever since she had got over keeping her mind made up that she didn't like Gyp, three years earlier, Annie had wanted to lead the usual domestic life with him. But he had come here to this wild hay meadow in the uncluttered bush of the western plateau at the end of a long search for some back corner of the world where he could live and let live and keep away from people who expected things of him; and as much as she had made herself precious to him and as gently and lovingly as she had made her expectations known to him, he had stuck to his unencumbered condition.

It hadn't been easy, and it had been and was unfair to Annie; Gyp knew that, and it was the reason for his feeling badly. Besides, it was all preposterous in the extreme, which he dealt with in his usual way, by not thinking about it very much.

Annie was more than simply attractive; she was overwhelmingly potent in all the irresistible charm of a young and supple and sexually eager woman. She was finely featured and lithe, and she made the most common movement, even the passing of a mug of tea, an excitement to watch in the graceful reach of her long, slender hands and willowy arms. When she walked she was pure silk, and however innocently she dressed, though she didn't always dress innocently, she could offer without the least contriving everything to drive a man to chaos in the secret places of his soul.

Gyp was not given to poetic utterances, even in silence to himself. The beauty in the world was evident to him, but he responded to it largely with an unexpressed contentment in its presence; if he said anything, it was rarely more than the equivalent of a "damn, but that's nice" and he'd say it of a flower or a mountain or a sunset or a well-coupled horse with about the same expression in every case.

And so when he had first seen Annie, he had not had words for the experience. He had trembled until he grew sufficiently accustomed to her to be able to be in Big Meadow's cabin at the same time with her without going utterly blank. Then he moved his defenses one stage farther: he very largely ignored her beyond the essentials of politeness.

Gyp had accepted since he first looked in a mirror that part of the unadjustable bad bargain of his existence was a most ineradicable homeliness, and he had accepted with it as he grew older the fact that he must live always without the pleasure of womankind.

He had imagined, in fact, that perhaps there was some strange redeeming justice that gave a man both a horror of being bound into domesticity with such God-awful looks at the same time that his bondage was about as remote a possibility as the freezing over of hell.

But still he was a man, and though he dreaded the bonds of commitment, he was powerfully enchanted by those unreachable mysteries of womankind and, like all sound men, had devoted perhaps the greater part of the lonely hours of his life to fantasies of beautiful women engaging him in the most intimate embrace.

But he was no fool, and believing absolutely that he would never enter that particular heaven on account of the colossal misfortune of his looks, he had never let himself introduce into his fantasies any living woman of his acquaintance, far less the sheer fire of a walking bombshell like Annie.

7

And so it was beyond understanding, absolutely, when, after he had been a couple of years at Upper Meadow and had only barely begun to be able to talk easily with her (and that only sparingly, given both their natures), that she came one night to his cabin and without the least warning or explanation made love.

It was completely out of the blue. Not a thing she had ever said or done before had given him any inkling that it was in her mind.

He had been totally swept away. Nothing his imagination had offered him in all the years of his expecting to do without forever had given him the least insight into this rapture.

She had not stopped moving from the moment she had taken hold of him until some long while later—Gyp had lost all sense of the passage of time—they had melted together in a burst of overpowering pleasure.

He drifted somewhere in a cloud of ecstasy, the light touch of her fingers leading him through ripples of afterglow. Once she had drawn his cheek very close to her lips and asked something that he didn't fully understand, about why he had not done that to her before. And, lost for the meaning of it, he had told her only the truth, that he had never expected that any woman would actually want him, and she had held him even closer.

He had been glad that she had not said any more, for he did not much care for the extent to which this intimacy threatened to lay his feelings out for inspection—by himself as well as Annie. Generally he preferred not to deal with his feelings, much less offer them as fare to others. It was easier to bury them and treat them, like most of life, with the amused indifference that Gyp had found necessary to make his existence possible.

It had been the next morning, in the very early hours, that the dilemma had risen up before him, and it had taken the form, precisely, of Annie loving and delicious beside him forever, accompanied by Annie large and pregnant and surrounded by children, the boys as homely as Gyp, the girls as lovely as their mother, all entreating him to enlarge the cabin and feed them and clothe them and never to look to the right nor to the left for nigh on thirty years.

So he had made love with her one more time before the dawn, then sent her home, and the next day he had ridden out to Lance Creek and caught the twice-weekly stage to Williams Lake. There he had fought through an embarrassment that all but rendered him dumb to have a most private discussion with the old gentleman in the pharmacy. In the past Gyp had never purchased from him anything more personal than worm pills for his horses and black leg vaccine for his calves. But the old gentleman had been very understanding and he rendered advice, reassurance, and merchandise with a warmth of a kind Gyp had not experienced since his father had shown him when he was a small boy how to take eggs out from under a cranky hen without getting his hand pecked.

Annie had seemed faintly surprised that Gyp should want to prevent the melting of their passions from resulting in her becoming pregnant—after all, it was she who would have the babies, not Gyp—and was even a little puzzled when, after her assurances that she really wanted to have children by him and her eager enticements to enjoy her without this unnatural restriction, he persisted.

But although Annie expressed herself fully and eagerly in her lovemaking, she expressed herself not much at all in words. They had by that time, it was true, taken to small exchanges of words. But these were comfortable in their avoidance of such issues as how one really felt, and Annie's few ventures into that risky ground had been dropped when Gyp had shown his complete reluctance to travel there himself.

So she had said nothing more about it, and Gyp had felt free to presume that it was tolerable to her, even if disappointing, that he put this limit on their relationship; and indeed, about that particular limit, he did not feel badly.

What he did feel badly about was that he never allowed her to stay in his cabin past the last hours of the night, into the new day.

He didn't presume to know why—Gyp Sandhouse didn't presume to understand even the most elementary things about himself—but the line between being in love with Annie Charlie and being responsible for her (and in some way bound to accede to her desire to have children) lay somewhere in the breaking of a new day.

If he let her stay on into breakfast cooking there would be implied a total conjugation, the fruits of which he would no longer be able to deny, and the burdens of which he could not bring himself to assume.

So even in the cold hours of a winter's morning Gyp would open the draft of the heater and throw on fresh wood so that Annie could rise and dress in a warm cabin. But rise and dress she must, and make the lonely walk home on the hard-packed trail in the snow between Upper Meadow and the cluster of cabins on the reserve.

Everyone, of course, knew about this unnatural behavior. Big Meadow Charlie knew, his wife knew, his daughters knew, his sons-in-law knew, his grandchildren knew, indeed, the whole village knew; for in the close horizons of a handful of people in a far corner of the world living largely in each other's hip pockets, as it were, everybody knows everything about everyone. But of course nobody would say anything because it wasn't their business, and Gyp wouldn't even discuss it with himself, much less anyone else. Even when Big Meadow came that only time to talk to Gyp about the advantages of a good woman in a man's cabin, he never once alluded to the idiocy of having half a woman when one could so easily have the whole of her.

And so even when Big Meadow Charlie came to Gyp's cabin to talk about something of specific importance, something of such importance as his illogical relationship with Annie, a long beginning silence and a half dozen false starts were needed; for in the precious friendship that had grown between the two men there was no place for a violation by running on at the mouth without cause for it.

Which was why on the day the old man came to tell him about the trouble with Moses Crease, Gyp knew it was a matter of life and death.

For the old man launched into it without one false start, and only barely having got settled in his chair.

II

It still took a long and circuitous telling, and it was made the longer by the infinite slowness of the words and the maze of events out of which the old, old Indian drew the long thread of his meaning.

It seemed, in the beginning, that it all centered on the Upper Meadow and did not concern Moses Crease at all, much less Gyp himself.

There was, first of all, the making of the reserves back in the last century before Big Meadow Charlie was born, when his father was still a boy and his grandfather was chief of the little straggling band of people who had taken up cutting hay and keeping scrubby beef cattle and motley horses to augment their hunting and their fishing and their drying of roots and berries.

11

It had been agreed and indeed intended by the agents of government that the whole of Big Meadow that could cut, you know, maybe three hundred tons of swamp grass, and Upper Meadow besides, which, though smaller, was better drained and had been made to grow half as much hay and far better hay at that on only a quarter as much ground; that both of these should be made into one reserve for the home village of the band.

But then there came the surveyor, and he measured out the ground; but he measured out only Big Meadow, and when the reserve was made it was made according to his plan.

Then the surveyor came back, but this time he was not any longer a surveyor, this time he pre-empted the land that is Upper Meadow, and by building a cabin, the old one that is now rotted away by the corral, and a fence around the hay ground, he got the land grant.

Which was all told without rancor, for men do what they do, and sometimes what another man does is to your disadvantage, but life is made in some measure of such things, and that was the way of it.

But the surveyor left and in time another man came, one Albert Crease, and for perhaps ten years he had the meadow, and he was a terrible man even by the generous and forgiving yardstick by which the people of Big Meadow measure their fellow man. He was cruel and stingy and mean and unfriendly, and totally by force he obliged a little crippled woman from the reserve to live with him, and she bore by him the boy Moses.

But he had taken the little crippled woman as an object for his meanness and to labor in his cabin, and the bearing of the child was an offense to his greed. He despised the child as he had despised the woman, and he abused them both in wild rages that betrayed how deeply he despised himself.

And then he left, abandoning the place, the woman, the child, everything.

But he left a terrible legacy in the child who, back with his mother in the fold of the reserve, grew to be the kind of man the little village, whose few souls lived out their lives in exactly seventeen cabins, could not contain without grief and disaster.

Gyp listened while the old man groped around to give unfamiliar meanings to the few words at his disposal, and he would have preferred very much not to listen at all, for he had met just a time or two in his life the kind of man Big Meadow told of Moses Crease growing up to be: a man without feeling, given to violence of a cold, indifferent sort, carried out without even the impetus of anger, and without any sense of the desperation with which other lives want to live.

As a boy Gyp had seen it in another boy who had killed a dog by inches over the course of a hot afternoon with pieces of rope and a stick. He had come on him at the end of it when there was nothing left of the dog to save and only a giggle of pleasure for Gyp's outrage.

Gyp had thrown up then, and he felt sick now and he wished the old man did not find it necessary to go on.

But the old man did, and the going on told of the fear of the little village and the cruelty of the beatings of the old and the weak—and finally of the killing of one lame man after a long and violent drinking party held, against the cripple's wishes, in his own cabin.

And even Gyp, who refrained from expecting anything from others with just the fervor that he wanted others not to make expectations of him, began silently to frame his indignation that the village let him do it. There were, God knows, enough men in those cabins to kill the bastard if that's what it took, and it seemed that nothing less would do.

13

Then, just as though Gyp had in some way conveyed this forming judgment against the village, Big Meadow dealt with it.

It was hard, he explained. Moses could not help what his father was, and that his father had hit him and tied him with chains and dragged him one time by his arm the whole way to Upper Meadow from the reserve where he had come one afternoon to play.

Moses could not help that, and Moses, you had to understand, belonged to the village. The people could not undo what the white man had done to him, but still they had to care for him as a boy and later, when he had become a man, they had to let him live among them, for where else could he live?

And as for anyone doing anything about him, well, you had to understand that the boys aren't very good at that kind of thing, they've never had to do that kind of thing before, and one at a time they're all scared of him and together they could never agree on doing something because they could never talk about it to start with.

The old man went on and Gyp, whose available vocabulary and command of the language far exceeded anything that others might have believed of him from his use of it, was amazed at the complexities of meaning the Indian put into the different arrangements he made of his handful of English words.

There was the hopelessness of calling the police, because until Moses had done something fearfully bad, in fact actually killed someone, you couldn't be sure enough of having him put away. And the fear of him taking revenge on individuals for speaking to the police about the beatings was far more immediate in its result than anything that could be hoped for by way of protection through the law.

Of course, after the killing the police had had to be called,

14

but because of the drinking and of what to Big Meadow was
the strange reluctance of the judge to realize what a threat to
life Moses would be for those who had been obliged to give
evidence, Moses was away only three years.

And now Moses had been back three years, and it had been
three years of intermittent hell for those he chose to pick on,
and though that had until now excluded Big Meadow Charlie's
family, the terror was growing to more than the people could
bear, and therefore the burden was becoming more than Big
Meadow could bear, and something had to be done.

Gyp struggled in the listening as the old man struggled in
the telling, and the face of Moses Crease settled in the eye of
his mind. It was a face he had seen as one of many in the
village, and he knew it by name and for the small exchanges
of the kind that maintain an uncommitting camaraderie
among men who by circumstance see each other in their
comings and goings but, by mutual choice, no more.

But he knew that he did not ever see him in the night. By
that same measure there were entire aspects of life in Big
Meadow's village that he had not ever seen and with which
Big Meadow had not, before, cared to burden him.

Then Big Meadow, having told it all, went on for some time,
perhaps another hour or two, and he regathered the ingredients of it all into different orders and different meanings,
and as he did so he drove Gyp around in the blind alleys of
the predicament: of the destruction of a boy who then grew
into a monster of a man but nonetheless belonged to the
same people he terrorized; of the impossibility for others of
taking a life, even though in time that life might take their
own; of how the police cannot prevent disaster, how they can
only come afterward and take away the one who caused it.

And imperceptibly at first, but with gradually growing
force, Big Meadow Charlie brought Gyp and his ownership
of Upper Meadow and the fact that he was a white man into

the picture he drew with his words, a picture which by that inclusion alone revealed the desperation of Big Meadow's dilemma, for never before had he found it necessary to place on Gyp the particular burden of that identity.

The picture clouded and cleared and clouded again in a tangle of ways that finally had Gyp so confused and spent through following it all that his eyes locked on the brown, wrinkled face with the sparse, grizzled stubble and the falling shock of gray-black hair.

Then, when he was so caught, Big Meadow Charlie made the picture clear again for the last and final time, and the simplicity of it was staggering.

He, Gyp Sandhouse, must do something about Moses Crease. It was, quite plainly, his responsibility.

III

Gyp continued to stare at the old man, as if by searching his face he could discover where it was that the seed of his responsibility had got planted in these entangling events, most of which had taken place before he had even heard of Upper Meadow. If he could find that place he would tear out by the roots the whole structure that Big Meadow had made on it, and hand it to him in shreds.

But the search afforded nothing for, his task of words quite finished, Big Meadow, motionless in his chair, stared silently again as always into the space of life's realities as this one old and unfathomable Indian knew them. As far as Gyp could tell, not one other soul in all creation knew finally what was seen there and Gyp, in five years of treasuring the simple presence of his friend, hadn't found it necessary, appropriate, or possible to conduct such an inquiry as might disclose it.

Although what the old man had done was by any logic preposterous, Gyp felt frantic to make denial. But only the feeblest of things occurred to him to say.

"Big Meadow, if I have learned one thing it is to stay the hell out of somebody else's trouble."

"That Moses Crease, he's gonna kill somebody anytime now, sure thing."

"Big Meadow, I am very busy. Three days before yesterday I opened the gate to let the water off'n the meadow. Two days after tomorrow she's gonna be dry enough to start mowing. I do not have time to get into this trouble about Moses Crease."

"She don't take much time, maybe."

That was the closest Big Meadow had come to actually saying the thing he had been talking about this long while. Nausea came to Gyp and passed over him heavily. When it left, Gyp was weak in his stomach and his knees. "Please," he objected faintly, "don't say anything like that again."

Then: "If I do anything like I think you have in mind, Big Meadow, she's going to take one hell of a lot more time than I have to spare. It's not the thing you are talking about that takes the time, it's after the police come to get me that takes the time."

"That time Moses kill that guy, he only gets three years."

Now the nausea passed over only lightly, and Gyp was appalled to discover that he was actually growing accustomed to this conversation.

"But that was an Indian killing an Indian, and he was drunk in the bargain. That is different. Even judges don't like to get into somebody else's trouble, and when you are a big white judge, I think Indians are mostly somebody else."

"You could get drunk too if she would help."

"I would get drunk too because I would *have to* get drunk. But I am not going to do her, Big Meadow." There, dammit, now it was out in the open and they were practically wallowing around in it, and Gyp wasn't even shaking in the hands any more.

"Some boys on the reserve, they lookin' after you cows and you hay. She all here okay when you comin' back. And Annie, she's still here when you comin' back."

"I am not going anywhere, therefore I am not having any coming back to do for my cows to still be here after. Or Annie."

There was silence for a while. Then: "That Moses Crease, he sayin' it now, he gonna kill somebody. Anytime now, she's gonna happen."

Futile ideas came to Gyp. Call the police, lay charges of threatening violence or whatever charges you lay in the case, find witnesses to say they heard him say it; but maybe it doesn't stick, and even if it does, how long before he's back, only months maybe.

The ideas left again. Gyp was glad to see them go. He was, after all, a realist.

Then Big Meadow said, not for the first time: "Upper Meadow sure is nice little ranch. He s'posed to be reserve, you know. He s'posed to be reserve but that surveyor, he's pretty crooked guy, I guess."

And for more than a brief moment it wound about Gyp's mind to make a bargain with Big Meadow. He'd give him the meadow and the buildings and the fences and the gear and he could do what he liked with it all, if he would only let Gyp off this business about Moses Crease. Gyp would pull out with a saddle horse and a pack horse and drive the cattle however far he must to find a buyer and get what he could for them. Maybe he could sell them to the Gill Ranch, and that would be only four days' drive at the most.

18

he repeated the crux of both their predicaments: "That Moses Crease, he gonna kill somebody. Any day now, she's gonna happen."

And Gyp sat still in the cabin for hours after the old man left. He did not even light the fire, and he was still sitting there, numbed by what was expected of him, when Annie came. She must have seen by his face in the diminishing light that her father had swept him into the terrible dilemma that was Moses Crease, for she said not a word but took him to bed with her, where they lay through the night in a way that they did for comfort, her back to him, his arm around her, his hand cupping her breast.

Only when she left in the morning did they mention the matter, and then in the most cursory way.

He said: "Your old man says I got to do something about Moses. What he says I got to do—I can't do it."

To which she replied: "We all got to do something about Moses. But none of us, we can't do it."

And the day that followed became the longest and strangest of Gyp's life. He went mechanically about the work of his two-dollar ranch in a trance, his mind going over and over the arguments by which Big Meadow Charlie had placed the burdens of life and death, which properly belonged Gyp knew not where, squarely on his shoulders.

And by so doing he found as many ways out as there were ingredients to Big Meadow's story, but these discoveries did not do him one damned bit of good.

They did not do him one damned bit of good because he was trapped, not by whether there was any logic in the roundabout arguments by which Big Meadow fixed responsibility upon him, but by the simple and unassailable fact that Big Meadow believed so completely, so absolutely and utterly, in the thing he had accomplished in his mind that nothing Gyp might say could create the least doubt.

When Moses Crease, any day now, did the thing that with all certainty he would do, it would be Gyp Sandhouse who had failed to take the one sure and pre-emptive step.

Gyp dreaded the irrevocable certainty of events.

IV

Gyp knew himself to be a simple man with simple wants, but he had not arrived at that perfect state of being without some difficulty.

There had been his mother.

She had been the hard-working and frustrated wife of a hard-working and contented homesteader of Jackson Creek in the Kootenay country of southeastern British Columbia.

She had wanted to be a serious student of drama and an actress of a most professional sort, but marriage had interfered.

She never forgave Gyp's father for this sidetracking of what would have been a brilliant career. He, on the other hand, suffered no anguish over this loss to the arts because, first of all, he didn't think there could really be anything seriously important in whatever it was she had wanted to do—she had constantly to explain it to him for the hundredth time, because he could never remember—and second, because he was one of only two people who knew whose idea it had been to make love one warm summer evening when her parents were out and he had come calling.

She might have been happy enough, too, except that the part of her that yearned for achievements of greater distinction than cooking and washing and sweeping and canning and having to shove wood into that monster of a kitchen stove even in hot summer weather, sought an outlet in her children.

And even that might have done the trick, vicarious though it was by its nature, except that the first son having grown up to be a student of law and the second having grown up to be a student of engineering, the third son grew up to be unmentionable within her hearing after about the fifth grade in school.

Gyp was the third son.

She had had hopes during the carrying of this last child that this would be the child to fulfill exactly that ambition she had given up in order to marry Gyp's father. The first two were already on the ladders of law and science. Their progress had been fired by the hothouse climate of their mother's ambition and the intense anxiety of the schoolteacher in hard times to keep her job—Mrs. Sandhouse was rural trustee with enormous influence over the affairs of the one-room school attended by the few children of the homesteaders who populated Jackson Creek.

But the hopes had died even in those first glimpses of the new infant. Though all new babies are for the most part wrinkled, red, and homely, it was painfully clear in this case that aging would not help, and though talent may be the first requisite of the stage, there are limits to what it may be expected to overcome.

Gyp must make it with his brains.

Gyp, unaware at first of the danger in exhibiting brains, learned to read with precocious ease.

His mother cooed over him.

He tossed off simple sums, intrigued by what he could do with ten fingers, an assortment of stubby pencils, and bits of eraser, which he increased in number by biting them in half.

His mother, seeing only the resulting progress in the sums, beamed her pleasure.

Then all came crashing down.

Gyp discovered that you did not read because and when you

felt like it, or do sums because it was so neat how you could go on to bigger numbers just by biting more and more pieces of eraser in half.

You read because you had to, and you read when you were told, and you added and you subtracted for the same reasons but without, henceforth, fingers and other numerous things to help you.

And not only that, but having done these things at imperious command each day, you then did them on test papers for the fixing of damaging remarks about you in report cards; and the most damaging of all was the recurrent one that said, "this boy is very intelligent but he will not do his work."

Gyp stopped performing in this particular circus, which he did not like at all, and stared vacantly out from beneath his protruding eyebrows at the trainer.

He saved his intelligence for contriving the lies that were necessary to his mother to sustain her belief that it was the teacher who wasn't hacking it, never Gyp.

A succession of teachers came and went from Jackson Creek. In time a legend developed in the teaching fraternity about the Sandhouse boy and his mother which, being a kind of nadir of desperation and injustice, was told repeatedly at teachers' conventions and at summer school for the higher certificate.

There followed then a most chaotic interval in which Mrs. Sandhouse undertook to teach Gyp herself, and all the ingenious fabrications of his tongue, all the carefully assembled words subtly put for their most emotive impact on his mother, were no longer of any use.

There was wailing and pulling of hair by Mrs. Sandhouse, both her own hair and Gyp's.

"My God!" she would cry, staggering from the task she had set herself, her hands clasped to her head. "That boy! He's stupid!"

Then: "Dear God, that boy! He *can't* be that stupid."

And finally: "My God, he really *is* that stupid. Oh, what will I do? It's driving me crazy."

Gyp stared impassively out from under the overhanging eyebrows, which had grown even more prominent in the intervening years, and said nothing.

His father said: "Aw, for Chrissake leave the little bugger alone. He'll get by. Look at me. I never made it out of grade four, and I'm doin' fine."

To which Mrs. Sandhouse made a face conveying the most utter, absolute, complete, and devastating disdain that her aspirations for the stage had equipped her to make.

And Gyp's father said: "Shee-eye-ucks!" and went back to where he'd left the big black team standing in the furrow where he was breaking new land for potatoes.

Gyp was then fourteen and quite able to compute all that he wanted when it came to cows or tons of hay, or how much he would go in the hole if his father paid him four cents apiece for fence rails and his mother charged him fifty dollars a month for board: the price of rails being his father's arbitrary figure, the price for board being what his mother had declared he'd damned well pay if he thought he was going to quit school and start common laboring for his living, and the number of rails he'd cut in a month being his own perfectly honest appraisal of how little he cared for work of any kind.

And he was quite able to read anything he wanted. In fact, secretly, he read quite a lot, though without conceding it any importance or really caring about it one way or the other. Certainly he did not admit anything of the kind to his mother, no brain capacity whatever, in fact, for fear that she would renew her resolve to make something of him, a process he did not wish to undergo any longer.

So he had continued to stare impassively out from under

those massive eyebrows until one day his mother made an observation in a totally new voice, a sort of intellectually detached voice, one that is used to observe very unusual phenomena that are of no personal significance whatever.

She said: "Do you know, he looks distinctively prehistoric. You could imagine him walking out of one of those caves after making a drawing on the rock."

And thereafter she ignored him absolutely, and if people mentioned his name in her hearing she would pretend that she did not know to whom they referred.

Gyp, much relieved, spent the next two years losing money cutting fence rails for his father, who forgave him all the debt when, at the end of that time, he found for himself a job on a labor gang with a large construction outfit that was building a new highway through the valley.

The job paid money like he'd never seen it before. He socked it away with a resolve that never left him through almost ten more years of doing work he didn't like, and abiding by the dictates of a time clock on a construction lot he couldn't bear, in company with men whom by and large he couldn't understand—for they drank and wasted money in such a way that failing the intervention of God they would be punching time clocks in and out of construction lots for the rest of their lives.

His bundle made, he did what he knew was the only intelligent thing.

He bought himself a pot hole meadow and a little herd of the kind of rangy beef cows that wouldn't be offended by the sort of life they'd have to live on the style of ranch Gyp Sandhouse would run, and all of this as far off in a back corner of midsection British Columbia as you could go without stumbling over the coastal mountains into the sea.

And there he reckoned to live in peace, doing just as little as he, personally, without anybody's help, asked of himself, and not a damned bit more.

Which was about where it was until he was affected by this awesome business about Moses Crease, and particularly by the unexpected turn of events that Big Meadow Charlie next reported to him.

V

Big Meadow had come to Gyp's cabin for the telling.

"That Moses Crease, I guess it happens pretty funny last night."

Gyp's mouth went dry and it was hard to make words, though there was surely something amiss in the old man's message. Pretty funny meant damned unexpected, and there was nothing to unexpect in the threat that was Moses Crease.

"What," Gyp asked hoarsely, "happened?"

"That boy, that Little Boy Charlie, he's havin' some kind trouble with that Moses Crease."

There was a pause, and in it Gyp thought first Oh God, not Little Boy Charlie, then second that he guessed it had to be somebody, then third that there was something profoundly wrong with the cool way that Big Meadow was letting out his bits of information because Little Boy was his own son, the youngest, unmarried, and by all accounts the least likely of anyone in the village to get in the way of violence. Even to be killed by someone as demented as Moses Crease you must have some capacity for coming into conflict. Little Boy Charlie didn't drink, argue, consort with women, or even but rarely venture out of his father's cabin after dark.

"Big Meadow, please don't play games with me. What in hell are you talking about?"

"That Little Boy, he's doin' it. That Moses Crease, he's kilt."

This left Gyp weak with relief and astonishment, and then the tragedy penetrated. If it had to be someone it was best it was Moses, but it was terrible that such a life had to be lived that its only solution lay in death. But you could not find words for such things; you could only talk around their edges.

"Little Boy. He's all right?"

"Oh, he's all right."

"How'd it happen?"

"He's doin' it with this big knife, you know. He's kill that Moses Crease."

Then Big Meadow paused, perhaps to look for some more words of English to fit this hell of a situation. While he paused, Gyp Sandhouse struggled against the smothering onslaught of things he desperately did not want to know about, far less become further involved in.

Asking how it had happened had been an enormous, monumental mistake, and Gyp jumped in with a barrage of his own words before Big Meadow could find even one more to open his mouth with.

"Look," he said, hurriedly, "don't tell me any more. I don't want to know any more. Already I know more than my gut can handle. I'm sorry about that because you maybe want to tell me but I've already had too much. I am a coward and I can't take any more."

And he just dimly perceived before he shut his mind to that as well, that his cowardice was not about the bloodshed. Bloodshed revolted him, but it had never frightened him. His cowardice was of becoming entangled again, of being somehow made responsible in the same bewildering way that before Moses had been killed, he had become responsible for the fact that Moses was still alive and dangerous.

It was like sending Annie home before the new day. If he could prevent any further knowledge of this entangling mess from reaching him, he could avoid being made responsible for it against his will.

And anyway he had already been told as much as his credulity could handle, for Little Boy was one of those anomalous people one sometimes sees who are so totally inept in the ways of their people that they cannot even survive without the constant support of others, much less rise in times of crisis to the heights of heroism.

Little Boy was immense and awkward, powerful but uncollected, and whenever he so much as moved, one held one's breath in anticipation of his falling over or bumping into something. He was as shy and timid as he was ungainly, and he had never learned more than the most elementary physical skills. He could ride only the gentlest of horses for fear of falling off, and if he drove a team, which he was rarely asked to do, it had to be a pair of old nags that would take whatever they pulled to wherever it was to go, even if they weren't being driven at all.

If he used an axe he'd cut himself, and if he lit a fire he'd get burned, and to make matters worse he'd been shipped off to the Indian Residential School near Williams Lake for most of his earlier years, with the unhappy result that what little chance he'd had to be a successful Indian had been thoroughly disrupted by the futile attempt to make him into a white man.

There hadn't been a preacher's chance in a cat house that anything he could have learned in the school would have enabled him to make a living in some other way, and it was beyond question that he could never make a living by the methods usual to the Indians of Big Meadow. He would perish by himself in the bush, quite apart from whether he could set a trap or skin a beaver. And so far as ranching was concerned, he could not be counted on even to put up hay without breaking into unusable pieces the simple equipment used at Big Meadow for that purpose.

Little Boy Charlie was, in short, a total and irredeemable failure for all practical matters, and Big Meadow expected quite happily to provide for him until, in his own extreme age, his other sons would take up the responsibility; quite happily not only because Big Meadow was the kind of man who meets kinship obligations cheerfully, but also because Little Boy was just naturally the most attractive man of little practical use that you could conceivably imagine. He wore a perpetual smile rather like a happy puppy wags his tail, and not just Big Meadow and his family but all the people in all the families that made up the little village looked out for him and were warmed by him and treasured his dependence on them.

There had been little in Gyp's life to lead him to be touched by gentleness in others, and he knew that these villagers were not by their nature inclined to make much demonstration of a tender sentiment; yet he was so moved by how they cared for Little Boy that it embarrassed him, and sometimes he turned away from the sight of it. Once he had seen a young boy take Little Boy's hand to give comfort when a runaway team, bolting through the village, had frightened him severely. Gyp had had to curse himself and look away to avoid his own emotion.

And now the unbelievable: with the village under constant threat by this monstrously dangerous man, Little Boy has, with a knife, done the thing that no one else could do.

You could hardly credit it.

But you must, for here is Big Meadow Charlie himself having just told you about it.

And, anyway, there were things that had to be done; and without really knowing quite why, Gyp sensed that he had better accept just that bit of responsibility that would ensure that they were done.

He asked: "What have you done with the body?"

"He's in back of church."

"You called the police yet?"

"Nobody call police."

"Well, you have to right away. Get someone to ride to Lance Creek, and they can phone from there. If you hurry there'll still be time for the police to come out from Williams Lake today. Where's Little Boy?"

"He's home."

"Well tell him to stay there till the police come."

Big Meadow did not move to go about these things, and while Big Meadow did not ever move right away to do anything, there was something in the not moving this time that suggested to Gyp that he'd been saying all the wrong things.

Gyp felt uneasy. "Big Meadow?"

"Yeh."

"What's wrong?"

They shared some more silence, and for longer than Gyp cared. Finally he broke it, though he had intended to leave that to Big Meadow. "Look, it's not my business. It's not my trouble, and I never wanted it to be my trouble, and I don't mean it to be my trouble now. It's your trouble, and I don't want to tell you how to look after your trouble."

He left that to see how it sat, but somehow it didn't seem to sit very well, and so he tried once more. "Big Meadow, the only reason I said those things about what you should do is I wouldn't like to see it get any worse than it is already. That's all. But it's not my trouble, so you handle it your way. I'm sorry I said anything."

And that turned out to be a very useful thing to say, for now Big Meadow disclosed how it was that he thought maybe he would handle this trouble that was his trouble, that Gyp wouldn't care to share with him.

"Maybe we don't need to call that policeman."

"What the hell do you mean, maybe you don't need to call that policeman?" Suddenly, without even thinking about it, Gyp had grabbed back a share of this responsibility that was so hateful to him.

"Maybe if we just bury that Moses, nobody going to miss him. Nobody going to ask where he's gone. If nobody ask where he's gone, policeman is not going to bother with him because policeman don't care much for Moses. Maybe it's just like Moses goes on long trip somewhere."

"Dammit, Big Meadow, the only long trip Moses ever went on was the one the police took him on. Moses was not the kind of man who goes on long trips. Moses didn't even know how to go far enough to get out of sight supposing he'd wanted to, and he didn't want to. And anyway, how are you going to bury him without letting the priest know? Big Meadow, I don't know exactly what kind of a Catholic you are, because that is the kind of thing I don't ask anyone, especially not my friends, but some of the people in that village aren't going to sleep well at night if you stick Moses in the ground without the help of the priest."

Then the clincher: "And Big Meadow, if you think you had trouble when Moses was alive and you think you got trouble now Moses is dead, you got nothing compared to the trouble you will have if you keep all this whole bad business away from the police and then they find out about it later."

Big Meadow thought for a while, and then let Gyp see just a little farther into the incalculable turns of his mind. "That was hard part, how we goin' to bury him without priest.

Goin' to be hard to get priest to understand about not telling policeman. Priest, he's not like Gyp. He don't understand very much my trouble. I'm not very good at talk, so maybe you goin' talk to priest."

"Not a damned chance. Big Meadow, it has gone absolutely far enough. You get somebody the hell down that road to the phone right away, and get the policeman in here, and then you just quit thinking. Turn it all over to the police before you get one more idea about it, and get us all in jail for the rest of our lives."

But still Big Meadow did not stir to go, and Gyp began to feel the kind of panic he sometimes got in a bad dream when he needed to run but his legs wouldn't move: it was imperative that something happen, and the something was Big Meadow telling one of the men to go to Lance Creek and the telephone —and yet be damned if you could get Big Meadow to move.

So Gyp waited to see what more was to come; and now he began to be totally apprehensive of Big Meadow's view of the events and what might or might not be done in response to them. He made ready to leap on the next proposal from his grizzled friend and flay it to pieces before it could breathe.

Finally it came: "That Little Boy, he can't make it in that jail, you know. He can't make it if he taken away from this people, you know. Some guys he can take it, you know, but not that Little Boy. He soft inside an' it kill him, I think, that jail for long time maybe some years."

Gyp flinched and looked away. He had not been ready for that. If he had known it was coming, he would still not have been ready for it. Never in all his life had he been or would he be ready to find answers for an old man who, unlike Gyp, would expose the matters of the heart so they might be faced like all other matters men must face, like hard winters or bad

33

weather for haying, or old, worn-out machinery and too little price for beef to buy anything better.

And he wondered, briefly, how many years in jail. Moses had got three, he remembered Big Meadow telling him. But there had been a party and a fight and Moses had been drunk when it had happened. There had been no time to make an intent to kill; it had just happened.

But Little Boy had taken the knife, and he never drank. And there must have been intent, born though it was out of the crescendo of fear that had gripped the whole village.

What would a judge understand of that?

What resolve, indeed, does it take to kill a man unless you are like Moses was, monstrous and without feeling? Gyp thought of his own impotence, his total and absolute inability even to consider such a course, and the forming of intent loomed large in his estimate of the issues that ultimately must be argued before a judge.

He could not cope, and in despair he turned on the old man. "Big Meadow, there is not a damned thing we can do about that. Little Boy has to go with the police, and there will have to be a trial, and you will have to tell the judge how it happened and hope for the best. I am sorry, but that is all. Now get the hell to that village and send someone to the phone, because otherwise I will go and phone myself, and I think when you are telling it all later it would be good to be able to say that you knew what was the right thing and you did it."

To which Big Meadow assented, but when he turned to go he said one more time: "He soft inside, that Little Boy, an' it kills him I think, in that jail long time, maybe some years."

And Gyp flinched again, but this time he did not let himself do any thinking.

Which probably made no difference anyway, for he would

never have foreseen that Big Meadow would choose such a precarious middle course.

He called the police, all right.

And when they got there he delivered them a body.

But Little Boy Charlie was nowhere to be found.

VI

This complication came to Gyp's attention when he arrived in the village late that afternoon at the request of the police. Annie had been sent to fetch him, but apart from saying that the police had arrived and that the sergeant wanted to talk to him, she had disclosed nothing more of the latest events.

Gyp knew the police had arrived, for he had heard and then seen the RCMP Beaver as it circled for a landing on Big Meadow Lake. And he'd reckoned the time of arrival of the police in the village because he knew how long it would take for a team and wagon to go and return by the long track along the meadow and through the willow swamp to the beach where the aircraft would nose in to let the men ashore.

And you could count on Big Meadow not to send the wagon until the plane had arrived.

So by the time Gyp had gone with Annie to Big Meadow's cabin to see the police, there was not much of the day left; just enough, in fact, if nothing delayed them, for the police to go back to the plane with the body and with Little Boy and return to Williams Lake before dark. Gyp had hoped they planned to do this, for if they stayed overnight they would stay at his cabin, and he really did not care for that.

He had cared even less for it after he had come to Big Meadow's crowded cabin where a score of villagers (mostly

Big Meadow's assorted family) and two police officers stood awaiting his arrival.

An efficient-looking Sergeant Petersen introduced himself, then his much larger and somewhat boyish-looking companion, Constable Shaw, and added: "You must be Sandhouse."

Which Gyp admitted to be the case, and waited. These were not his matters that lay here to be settled. He would have preferred by a long way to have been left out of them.

There was an awkward pause, but Petersen did not let it hang on too long. "I'd like to speak with you alone," he said, in the quiet, deliberate tones of one who exercises an unquestioned authority. "Let's go outside."

They did so, and Petersen went directly to what Gyp liked least. "What do you know of this business?"

And Gyp looked steadily at him for a moment without replying, for it was a hell of a question. About the events, damned little, in truth. About that old conniver, Big Meadow Charlie, and what went on in his mind, too much, in truth. But was he bound to deal with that? He decided not.

"No more'n I can help, which isn't much," he finally offered. "Big Meadow Charlie doesn't talk much, and I don't ask him questions."

It was then that Petersen had replied in efficient, abrupt summary: "Well, I *have* asked him questions, and it hasn't been very useful. In fact, I only know there was a fight, one Little Boy Charlie killed Moses Crease with a knife, and now Little Boy Charlie is nowhere to be found. Nobody admits to knowing where he is or even when they last saw him." A note of sarcasm came into Petersen's voice: "Can you imagine a whole, entire village not knowing when they last saw someone who was in this house last night but isn't here today? Of course, I haven't questioned everyone, but that's the story I'm getting, and I don't expect it will change."

Gyp could imagine a whole, entire village not knowing

damned nearly anything Big Meadow decided they should live in ignorance of, but he decided not to offer that.

And now, to Gyp's relief, Sergeant Petersen spent some little while thinking, a few bits of it out loud. It gave Gyp a chance to incorporate this latest information, this unavailability of Little Boy, into the muddle that already occupied his mind.

"I think," Petersen said slowly, forming the plan as he spoke, "I'll take the body out now. I've just got time. And I'll leave Shaw here to pick up Little Boy when these people make up their minds that they don't want to go to jail for hiding him out. He can phone me when he's got Little Boy. Is it far to the phone?"

"Five miles. Hour's ride unless there's some panic."

"I see. Better yet then, I'll just come back in three or four days. If Shaw has Little Boy it won't matter if he has to wait that long, and if he hasn't by then, I'll want to talk to these people again myself, anyway. Can Shaw stay at your cabin?"

"I guess he'll have to."

Then Petersen moved back to the question of Little Boy, and Gyp would have preferred more questions, like how far is it to the phone. But it was Petersen who owned the initiative, and he asked: "Little Boy must be in the village or close by, don't you think? He wouldn't likely have taken to the woods."

Gyp did not wish to answer that, because he had tried already to answer it for himself without any satisfaction. So he said: "I don't know." But that was not altogether true, because he did know that it was powerfully unlikely that Little Boy would have taken to the woods, and his dissatisfaction came from wondering where in hell, in fact, did Big Meadow Charlie have Little Boy hidden. About that Gyp felt unaccountably uneasy.

Petersen asked another question, just as Gyp had begun to

hope he'd quit. "What do you know about Little Boy? He dangerous?"

Gyp shook his head. "Little Boy Charlie wouldn't stand up to a fly over his breakfast. He's the last man you'd expect would have tackled Moses Crease. I guess he only did it because Moses was getting so vicious he was bound to kill somebody some day." After which Gyp shut up, astounded at his own volubility.

"Figures," Petersen said. "We knew Moses. Pathological killer. But you can't take the law into your own hands. We want Little Boy, and one way or the other we'll get him."

And just for a moment a wave of indignation bordering on anger swept over Gyp, crowding out the predominant wish to be left out of this business, and he almost (but not quite) cried out against the stupidity of that cliché, you can't take the law into your own hands. What else, for God's sake, *can* you do when you live where the law only exists long after the outrage of violence has happened?

But the feeling ebbed, and for a while the two men pondered each other, Gyp beginning to sense the person within the neat, spotless uniform. What he sensed was what he often sensed in men who possessed a secure place in the established life that Gyp avoided: that whatever they thought or said or did was without question in their minds wholly correct, and even that certainty, much less the substance, was by its nature a judgment on the unestablished ways of men like Gyp.

Gyp did not, of course, give the feeling words in his mind —Gyp seldom gave words to any of his feelings—but it further occurred to him that if Petersen knew, as in time he would, that he, Gyp, was sleeping with Annie Charlie, the man would fix an ineradicable measure of unimportance to him on account of it.

38

But Sergeant Petersen's pondering of Gyp must not have been quite so disapproving at that moment, whatever Gyp expected of it in the longer run, for when he spoke again it was to share a confidence with him.

"I should mention something to you about Shaw. He tends to dramatize things. Gets them out of proportion. Don't let him make some kind of cockeyed adventure out of this. He'll talk to you about it, and if he starts to be unrealistic, pull him back to earth."

Responsibility again. Dammit. But Gyp said nothing and merely nodded; Petersen, treating it as conclusive, said that that was about all, and went back into the cabin.

Gyp followed and listened while Petersen explained that he was leaving at once with the body, that Shaw would be staying, and that he fully expected that Little Boy would be turned over to Shaw before he returned in three or four days.

The last thing he said was a repetition of an earlier warning: that anyone proven to have helped Littly Boy hide out would be liable for a penalty up to half the penalty that would apply to whatever Little Boy was finally convicted of —and that in view of the fact there'd been a killing, the people would be well advised to think of that as meaning a solid stretch in jail.

And while Petersen spoke, Gyp's eyes never left Big Meadow's face, but Big Meadow registered absolutely not one shred of a tremor. Gyp earnestly wished that he could be so cool in such complicity if the need should ever arise, which, by God, he would ensure it did not. Yes sir, you could count on that. Not in this world, not Gyp Sandhouse. No possible way.

And after Petersen left and Shaw went outside to measure and make a sketch of the steps and the ground in front of Big Meadow's cabin where, it was now apparent to Gyp, the killing had been done, he had an opportunity to ask the old man what the hell had been going on.

And for a while he looked at Big Meadow and Big Meadow looked at him, and in the wordlessness of this exchange Gyp realized that however much he wanted to keep this old bastard out of trouble, and however much he worried about the safety of that near idiot, Little Boy Charlie, knowledge had become a dangerous thing, and he wanted none of it.

So he grinned and he shrugged, and this felt very good because he had not found anything fit to grin about for at least three days. In fact, it felt so good he tried it again, and this time the faintest glimmer of a smile crept over the old man's face, and he added to it a very conspiratorial nod of his large gray head.

And there, at that point, Gyp panicked and got at once out of that cabin, for he had realized suddenly that Big Meadow's supply of that dangerous commodity, knowledge, was enormous, and he must just be waiting for the first or any good chance to pass some of it along to his friend.

It was later that evening that Big Meadow managed it, and he didn't have to say a word or even be there. He had simply arranged events so that the exchange was sure to take place.

VII

The boyishness of Shaw was rather remarkable because, on closer notice, Gyp realized that Shaw was by no means a stripling. If anything, he was older by a little than Gyp, and it had been something in his manner and his movements that

40

had conveyed that impression, not of youthfulness exactly, but of a young boy's exaggeration of what went on around him.

In Big Meadow's cabin he had searched among the faces that surrounded him as though they kept the secrets of a great intrigue of international proportions, far beyond the rather mundane question of where the hell was Little Boy Charlie, though he had left anything needing to be said to his senior in the Force.

But now in Gyp's cabin, where they had come since there wasn't enough left of the day to do anything more, he grew voluble and demonstrative. His face and hands were expressively mobile, and to the taciturn Gyp, whose own nature was more compatible to Big Meadow and his long silences than to anyone else he'd ever known, the experience was startling.

Shaw had settled himself at the table while Gyp built a fire for the cooking he must do before they could eat.

There'd been an expressively silent moment or two while Shaw collected his imagination, his head nodding knowingly, his mouth set in a resolutely sleuthing line.

Then: "This man Little Boy—guess he'd be pretty dangerous." It was an assertion more than a question, and the emphasis had been on the "pretty." Shaw's eyes had squinted a little as he had said it, his mind measuring the importance of this fact in the life and death case that rested now in his hands alone.

Gyp managed to say, rather ineffectually: "I wouldn't exactly say that."

Which was splendid by Shaw, for it created the opportunity for him to say, most sagely: "*Those* are the worst." And his head still nodding in that specially knowing way: "The ones you wouldn't think would kick a dog. *They're* the ones to watch out for. *They're* the killers."

And the way he said "killers" completely robbed the word

of any horror it might have had for Gyp, indeed should have had for Gyp in his sense of the tragedy of the past days and years of Big Meadow Reserve. There was something entrancing in this quite unreal perception of people and events that caught you up in it and made you join in its pursuit. "Yes," Gyp said, slowly, "you might be right." He wasn't sure that he didn't nod his head a little himself in that very knowing way.

Shaw rose to his feet to pace the floor, his hands clasped behind his back, his head thrust forward intently. On his way by Gyp at the stove he stopped to lean close to Gyp's ear, and in little more than a hoarse whisper he let him in on another skillfully detected fact: "And that Big Meadow Charlie. You watch him. *He* knows a whole lot more than he's letting on."

That one was too close to home for Gyp to add to—except inwardly, where he groaned to himself, "My God, yes, and don't I wish the old bastard would tell it all to Sergeant Petersen but not, please God, to me."

Then back by the table again Shaw spun on his heel and in carefully spaced, deliberate words, he enlarged on the gravity of the matter.

"I'll tell you what I think. I think that Big Meadow Charlie is more involved in this than meets the eye. *He's* the one who's behind it all. He probably put Little Boy up to it and now he *has* to keep him out of sight or he might talk. He'd spill the whole thing."

Gyp allowed to himself that you certainly had to admire a theory as perceptive as that. No two ways about it, no sir. But not yet having as much experience at this sort of thing as Shaw, the most he was able to say in response to it was: "Pardon me while I get some potatoes."

Whereupon he lit a lantern, then heaved back the bearhide, opened the trap door, and crawled down the short ladder into the seven-foot hole beneath the floor, where he stored his vegetables.

It was at the point that his eyes, growing used to the dim outlines exposed by the lantern in the cellar, made out the huge shape of Little Boy reclining in the potato bin, his face responding with a warm smile to this intrusion into his hide-away, that Gyp heard Shaw call after him with the clarity of a horse bell on a cold morning: "Say, you got any idea where that old man would hide out that boy of his? If we could figure that out, we could sew this thing up."

That was the moment, no question of it. Then was the time to say yes, you're damned right I do, and then say to Little Boy, come on now, it's the only way and you have to go; and Little Boy would have done as he was told as eagerly as he would do anything anyone asked of him in that implicit trust he had in all people, as though when you are so unable to discover the simplest courses for yourself and must depend forever on others, all men are your father, and you do as they tell you.

Yes, that would have been the moment, the moment in which Shaw waited for you to answer him and Little Boy looked at you in the dim light of the lantern with that eager, ever-present, trusting smile, and you knew that he did not, could not possibly have the least notion of what it was that had been taking place, even in whatever unbelievable freakish circumstance must have let him do that deliberate act about which Gyp Sandhouse dared not even think.

But somehow it crowded into that all too short moment that insisted on an answer up the short ladder and out the trap door into the cabin to the policeman who already was making the forewarned cockeyed adventure out of Little Boy's disappearance; it crowded into that moment that Big Meadow Charlie had understood more than any of them when he had said, "It kills him I think, that jail for long time, maybe some years."

And perhaps if the moment had been just a little longer Gyp might have managed to find a right way, though more likely in fact there wasn't one.

As it was, he said loudly: "Hell no. I haven't the least godamned idea where Big Meadow would hide that boy."

After which he made a hushing sign to Little Boy, tossed half a dozen large potatoes up through the trap door to land noisily on the floor above, drew himself up the ladder and out, closed the trap, threw the bear hide back over it, then gathered up his potatoes, which he set to peeling hurriedly for supper.

His hands shook and the potato peeler made a rattling sound between swipes.

But, deep in the mysterious processes of solving this unfathomable case, Shaw paid him no heed. In time Gyp's hands steadied and his nerves adjusted to the new level of intrigue at which he now must operate.

Shaw reached a point of decision, a settled conclusion, a crystallization of truth out of the shrewd sifting of facts which, once fixed, marked the point of departure for another phase in the investigation.

He declared: "He wouldn't leave him in the village. That would be too obvious, and too many people would know about it. No, I'll tell you what he'd do." The measured cadence came back into his words. "He'd hide him out someplace not too far away."

"Believe you're right," Gyp acknowledged. There. It wasn't such a hard game to play after all. With a little practice he could do very well at it.

But to do well at it he would have to find the dexterity to match the sudden shifts in speculation that Shaw's imagination brought into the reckoning. For no sooner had Shaw sleuthed it out that Big Meadow Charlie would have hidden Little Boy not too far away, than somewhere between the potatoes and the tea he abandoned that proposition for one that was patently absurd by comparison: that Little Boy had headed into the bush, had gone out on the trail on horseback, had taken it on the run.

The shift had come while Gyp was still making what show he could of puzzling on that earlier matter, that question of where, not too far away, would Big Meadow Charlie hide Little Boy. Perhaps Gyp had been too occupied with making his own steadfast gaze into the imagined mysteries of the case to pay enough attention to the glazed look that passed for a long moment over Shaw's face and out of which afterward the constable had come alive with excitement. In any event, Gyp was so surprised at the new turn that he almost failed to keep pace with it.

"That's it!" Shaw had exploded. "We'll take horses and track him down!"

"Track him down?" If Little Boy Charlie had been hidden in some handy place by Big Meadow, how the hell would you track him down? Men's boots on dry trails or cropped grass do not leave tracks, and doing the job on horseback wouldn't make it any easier.

"Sure," Shaw said with enthusiasm. "He's taken to the bush on horseback, that's what he's done. We'll go and track him down. Right away, before Petersen comes back. You've got some saddle horses, I guess? We'll need a tracker."

"A tracker?"

"Yeh. A tracker. You always have a tracker. One of the older Indians who trusts the Mounties. Sort of like a scout."

"Oh, I see." And Gyp made the transition without any further problem, because he had seen a picture once (in a book he was pretending for his mothers' greatest anguish that he couldn't read) of a red-coated Mounted Policeman and a blanket-coated Blackfoot Indian with their horses reined up at a fork in the trail. The Blackfoot was pointing down to the tracks on the ground before them. The Mountie, a square-jawed man of great determination, was visibly measuring the tracks and the words of his tracker together; he was about to declare his next move—and whatever it would be, he would always get his man.

So Gyp then saw into the trance behind the glazed stare that had held Shaw silent for those few moments, the meaning of which he almost had missed, but which now he took hold of in all seriousness: "We can be out of here a little after day-break. I got two good saddle horses and an old pack mare in the yard. But I don't know about any of those guys from the reserve for a tracker. Maybe I'll just have to do that part myself."

Gyp feared for a moment that in Shaw's determination to stick by tradition he might respond to Gyp's proposal to be the tracker as though Gyp had offered him an American tourist for the job. But Shaw had grown ecstatic with the sudden availability of the main ingredients—the fugitive, the trail into the timbered hills, the necessary horses—and the substitution of a two-dollar rancher for a sagacious old Indian tracker was not, apparently, beyond his imagination to tailor into the drama.

And so it was settled, and there passed then for Gyp a strange evening in which he listened on the one hand to Shaw's boyish enthusiasm for this manhunt they had schemed, an enthusiasm that bore no more relationship to the realities the chase would entail than the chase itself to the fact of Little Boy's presence in the cellar below them; and listened on the other hand constantly into the silence below the cabin in fear that Little Boy, constrained in the darkness, would finally have to move about to relieve his stiffening muscles and would bump into things in the night.

The one kind of listening interfered mightily with the other. It would have been difficult enough for Gyp, given as he was to living out the days and the events of his own life without perceptible enthusiasm, to pay adequately responsive attention to Shaw's excited questions about the horses, the saddles, the means of packing, what outfit they'd take, the camps they'd make; but when he had to listen to all that greenhorn speculation pacing animatedly about the cabin out of one side of his mind while he nursed his anxiety about Little Boy's capacity to hold silence with the other, it was damned nearly more than even his store of imperturbability could handle.

He finally dealt with it all by saying they'd better go to bed, they were going to be up pretty early in the morning. But it wasn't clear that this was any improvement, for Gyp couldn't make up his mind whether he wanted Shaw to keep talking even though the talk was going to loosen the hinges of Gyp's sanity completely if it went on much longer, or whether he'd like him to shut up and try to sleep even with the consequent risk that if Little Boy began thumping about there'd be no other sounds in the night to give him cover.

Gyp could not remember in the morning whether Shaw had still been talking when finally he'd gone to sleep; he only knew that somehow they'd all got to sleep, Little Boy as well, he presumed. It was as though he'd woken again, not into a proper day in this damned strange life he now lived, but into a vividly real dream; but the dream was not the sort, unfortunately, that, by an act of sheer willful consciousness, you could penetrate and reorder if it got out of hand on its own. This one seemed irrevocably committed to ordering itself and to preventing Gyp from either fixing it up along more tolerable lines or escaping it altogether.

He rolled out early to make breakfast and got himself and Shaw out of that cabin as quickly as he damned well could; but he did it all with a profound feeling that it could have no useful result whatever.

VIII

It was easy enough to account to Shaw for the proposition that they should go by Big Meadow Charlie's place to tell him what they were planning on doing. For whatever Big Meadow had had to do with the disappearance of Little Boy, in the limited society of the Big Meadow Reserve and Gyp's place, the unannounced disappearance of Gyp and Shaw would suggest conclusions as deducible as if they had been announced in church. You might as well play above board and declare your intention.

It was not so easy for Gyp to account to Big Meadow Charlie for what he was doing or was about to do when, reined up in front of Big Meadow's cabin with his pack mare in lead and Shaw mounted on his spare saddle horse there beside him, he looked at his old friend, who had come out onto his front steps to see what it might be that was happening next in the world.

And it was made substantially more difficult to account for when Big Meadow Charlie, whose sense of humor was as unfailing as it was contained, grasped at once the absurdity that was Shaw, and with little more than a flick of his eyes and a hint of a laugh over the creases of his face, conveyed unmistakably to Gyp that whatever it was Gyp had in mind, it had to be preposterous.

Gyp spared a comprehensive glance at Shaw, then himself.

It was momentary, and so deftly done that Shaw was not aware of it, but still it was observant, and it was the first perceptive look Gyp had taken at him since he'd got him mounted with some difficulty back at the corral at Upper Meadow—and, lord, you had to admit, Big Meadow was onto something.

There is some ingredient in the limp posture in the saddle of men like Big Meadow Charlie or any of a score of others in his village—or like Gyp himself, for that matter—that says of them that if they weren't actually born astraddle of a horse in leather, they've spent so much of their lives there that they have become all but an extension of the horseflesh itself.

There is nothing proper about the way they ride; you will not, for instance, find it anywhere written about in books in the way that you will find the correct seat for taking the jump as prescribed by the British Horse Society. It is just that they ride because they must, because it is an ingredient of their lives, and they have not thought much about it, if at all. They sit loosely, sometimes with a resigned acceptance of the tediousness of so much of it; but they are forever relaxed in that contained way that lets them stay in the saddle however suddenly and viciously a good horse or a bad one might change direction and location in the fifth of a second when their mind is on anything else but the contrariness of horseflesh.

But they do not think about it or analyze it or understand it. They just do it, and it only comes clear to them that there must be a way they do it when they see something as ludicrous by contrast as Gyp Sandhouse was drawn by the observant humor of Big Meadow Charlie to witness in Constable Shaw on that particular morning.

For Gyp had to admit to himself, as quietly as he had completed the summary glance, that it was indeed a sight.

In fairness to Shaw you had to admit as well that it began

with that damned silly horse. He was tall and mostly black but with one patch of white, which started where it should have, in the middle of his forehead, then veered off to slash across one eye, which in some singular way lacked direction and seemed to be looking anywhere but where it should be. He was angular, too, this horse, and his ears fell out sideways and were at least half as long again as they had any business to be, and the moment he was let stand he would shift his weight onto one hind leg in order to let the other go slack, then droop his head and close the whole of the good eye and half of the misdirected one as well.

Gyp only owned the horse because he'd come with the place. Even at that he was a nuisance, because anytime he got out of the yard at Upper Meadow he'd head off through the bush the thirty miles to Pascal's Lake, where he'd been raised on a long-deserted homestead of even less proportions than Upper Meadow. And Gyp would have let him go except that he was getting old now, and come winter he'd starve to death when the snow got too deep, as it did at Pascal's Lake, to paw easily through to the sparse swamp grass that grew in the meadow there. Which would have been fine, too, because Gyp already had more and better horses besides this stray-eyed gelding than he could conceivably use, but ownership of a horse conveys with it the onerous responsibility of looking after it as well. So there the cayuse was, forever eating grass and hay that Gyp could ill afford, and looking at Gyp with that two-directional stare that Gyp preferred, generally, not to return.

And so your antecedent condition of being almost horseflesh had to go a long way back and be thoroughly accomplished if you were going to sit on that gelding and make it look a sensible undertaking; for Shaw it was, obviously, an utterly hopeless task.

For Shaw's singular method of straddling a horse was to sit

bolt upright and let the rest look after itself; at least as nearly as Gyp could deduce that must have been it, but then Gyp was no hand at the analysis of such things, this being the first time in his life that he'd seen anything to even make him think on the matter.

Shaw sat bolt upright, ramrod straight, and his ears (which, like the gelding's, were rather oversized, and which stuck outward from his close-cropped head) were accentuated by the RCMP forage cap, which by itself seemed anomalous as a piece of riding dress. It was certainly a long way from the broken-down, wide-brimmed felt hats that the men of Big Meadow employed to shed rain and fend off the wind.

And then somehow, by turning his heels outward, he contrived to look pigeon-toed. That in itself, since his feet were separated by the whole girth of the gelding, would have put him somewhere short of being taken seriously. But added to that were the long blue trousers with the yellow stripe down the side and the Sam Browne belt and the immaculate khaki shirt with the epaulets, all managing to be worn by this one boy of a man in such a way as to be incongruous beyond any believable point.

And there he sat, bolt upright, with the reins firmly clutched in both his hands, dead center in front of his stomach. By the time Gyp had taken it all in and returned his eyes to meet the sparkle in Big Meadow's—a process that couldn't have lasted for more than a second or two—the task of accounting to his friend for why he was there and what he might hope to be doing had got away quite beyond reach.

He rather wished he hadn't set it for himself.

But there wasn't much avoiding it; for if there was one straw of reason in this whole elaborate caper with Shaw, it was that it got Shaw the hell out of Gyp's cabin while Little Boy was stowed beneath it. But nothing would be accomplished by that if by the time they returned there, Big

Meadow did not have Little Boy out again. And all of this had to happen, it seemed in the nether regions of Gyp's gut, where evident things tended to make themselves felt, before Sergeant Petersen got back from Williams Lake.

But what of this grizzled old Indian who seemed to know so little and yet so much, who knew things indeed that Gyp earnestly did not want to know, if the things he had demonstrated already were any indication of what still lay in his conniving mind?

Yes, what of him indeed? How do you tell him what you want him to do, and how, having told him, do you know if he understands? And then, supposing you feel assured of that, what hope have you that he will *do* what it is that you hope he understands of what you're going to try to find some way to tell him?

Especially when, before he has said a word on this early hour of a summer's morning as he stands on that damned silly bit of a front step of his cabin looking at you, he has already passed judgment on your present enterprise, and found it wanting beyond redemption.

All you have done thus far is put that man on that horse, and yet, by God, you have already washed out.

Gyp made words, the best he could manage: "Big Meadow, we are going out to look for Little Boy. We will be gone maybe three days."

And then in silent pleading, Big Meadow, please help me to pretend that it is possible that he is out there someplace, and that I might cut his track and fetch him in a day or two. I know that is a lie, but please do not look at me as if I were crazy. There really is a good reason for this game I am playing.

"What you could do Big Meadow, I don't suppose you got any idea where Little Boy *is* right now, but suppose you happened to find out while we're gone, you could tell him it's no good trying to hide, and you could keep him right here at your place till we get back."

That is a lie too, Big Meadow, but that lie is just as much your lie as it is my lie, so don't look at me like that anymore. Because if you want me to pretend your game, you have to pretend mine.

"Matter of fact, Big Meadow, just in case we don't have any luck ourselves, I think maybe you ought to try to find out where he is and get him here into your place." Gyp leaned very heavily on the getting him here into your place, because that was the aspect of this particular game he wanted Big Meadow Charlie to play at the hardest.

But as he had known all along would be the case, you could not tell from looking at him what Big Meadow had let himself get out of all that doubletalk. To spare himself further embarrassment, Gyp turned his horse to go. The lanky gelding with the misdirected eye started up too, and because they were making a westerly direction, set off with enthusiasm.

Gyp reined up just once to look back, and because the lanky gelding kept on going, Gyp debated momentarily about having one quick word privately with Big Meadow, who still was standing on his steps not forty yards away. He could quickly ride back, say his piece, then catch up with Shaw—and Shaw wouldn't have to suspect that it was anything more than an afterthought to what had already been said in his presence.

But while he watched in that moment of debate with himself about whether to make further words or not, he saw his old friend, unmistakably, shake with laughter from head to foot. It was nothing audible, just a slow, rhythmic shaking of his great body and a slight tilting back of his head to make way for his escaping delight.

Gyp glanced back and forth again between the fast-walking gelding and his too-godamned-much-amused friend, and then abandoned the idea of more words altogether.

It wasn't, he said to himself, that he might not have got anywhere with Big Meadow. It was just that if he didn't get in front of that gelding pretty quickly, he'd take Shaw to Pascal's Lake before Gyp would get another chance to catch him up.

IX

It was July of 1874, the founding year of a great tradition in the conveyance of British justice into a wild and lawless land.

The place was Fort Dufferin, and the compelling strains of martial music filled the air as the fledgeling Force moved out to westward on the long march into a vast territory which, for some years previous, had been freely plundered by American whiskey traders and desperados, who created havoc and desolation among its Indian inhabitants.

The men of the North West Mounted Police, tightly disciplined, rode tall in the saddle, their heads up, ever alert, their scarlet tunics brilliant in the sun and visible for miles across the open prairie.

And so, too, rode Shaw, in this latter-day rerun of the glory of the Force, tall in the saddle, head up and ever alert. It was a little difficult, this head-up stuff, because the nondescript rancher on scout duty in front of him was barging through the brush in a most disorderly way, and the branches seemed to swing back just in time to catch him full on the cheek.

54

Being alert could have been easier too. It is hard to be alert when about all you have time or visibility to keep track of is the hind end of the horse in front of you.

But the two-dollar rancher was alert to several things without difficulty, things such as where he'd better arrange to be by the time Sergeant Petersen would be back to Big Meadow, and where he'd like not to have been at all for most of the previous week.

However, what he was mostly alert to just now was the fact that he could only go on riding in a big circle around the vicinity of Big Meadow, pretending to look for fresh saddle horse tracks leading outward, for about two hours at the outside. By then he'd have crossed every one of the half dozen trails that went places from Big Meadow, and he'd either have no track at all or he'd have a track, but it wouldn't be left by Little Boy going someplace on horseback.

Of course, he could still make believe on the strength of such a track—except that more sooner than later, with his kind of luck, he would meet the horse that had made the track, and it would be evident that the horse was not carrying Little Boy.

Fort Whoop-up was the base camp of the iniquitous whiskey traders, gun runners, and murderers foraging northward out of the lawless American West. Its consummating audacity was that it flew the American flag, deep in Canadian territory.

And it was solidly built, virtually impregnable to any weaponry likely to confront it. It had been built by men whose modus operandi revolved solely around what could be accomplished—taken, destroyed, defended—by brute strength.

But the North West Mounted Police did not seek stature by brute strength. Indeed, if they had, with the paucity of numbers allowed them in their establishment—three hundred

*men to bring order to that whole vast territory west and north
of Fort Garry—the only stature available to them would have
been a posthumous and futile heroism.*

They sought stature by more subtle methods.

*Assistant Inspector McLeod left his company camped a dis-
tance off. Alone but for a métis interpreter he rode, scarlet-
coated and fearless, to the portals of the fort and hammered
commandingly on the gate.*

*It could not be helped, and it was perhaps just as well, that
the fort by then was occupied by only one old man and a
handful of Indian women, the host of renegades having
deserted the place days before on hearing of the approach of
the red-coated column.*

Already, Constable Shaw had prepared for how he would
bear himself upon the final cornering of Little Boy.

They would doubtless come on him making his last stand
in an abandoned cabin somewhere deep in the trackless bush.

They would see the smoke from his fire rising from the
rusted remnants of the stove pipe through the sod roof, his
exhausted horse tethered in the long grass of the clearing,
lame, with hardly enough strength to feed.

It would be then that the rancher, who unfortunately now
was rather more in charge of things than was really appropriate—the role of tracker and scout implied a partnership of
competence with the Mountie in the craft of the manhunt,
but not quite this total assumption of decisions that seemed
here to be the case—it would be then that he would turn to
the Mountie and confess his distaste for this dangerous business.

And Shaw would, as a matter of course, accept that. Courage is not, after all, equally apportioned among men. And, in
any case, what would then remain to be done belonged

properly to the Force, not to the tracker. So Shaw would give him the leave he would want to stay hidden in the trees, while Shaw would ride out alone into the clearing and up to the cabin.

He would call out to the man to give himself up, and never once would there be a question of force. He would ignore his own weapon completely, and by his total indifference to danger, by his exhibiting so plainly that for him no danger existed, he would so awe the fugitive that Little Boy would come out of the cabin and, on Shaw's reaching out for it, would give up his rifle.

The rancher wished to God the policeman would do a better job of keeping up. Although he knew there were some anomalies to be faced in the matter of tracks, he didn't want to put off forever getting onto a decent trail on account of that.

The men of that fledgeling Force, having established their posts in the far reaches of a vast territory, went out one by one to bring law, order, and justice to white and Indian alike, without favor of any kind. They offered a helping hand to any law-abiding man, and they sought by their constant patrols into the far reaches of the frontier to prevent crime from being committed. They saw this as the much preferred duty to apprehension and prosecution afterward.

Still, when some impudent man was so rash as to do some wrong within the territory, then however far the chase, however small the transgression, however harsh the weather or deep the snow, the lone Mountie, aided by his loyal Indian or métis companion, would press unremittingly toward one unfailing end: that justice be done.

Come hell or high water, the Mountie always got his man, and on the trail of the fugitive, he was indomitable.

The relentless tracking down was the centerpiece of the action.

Constable Shaw was much relieved that at last they were on a well-defined trail where he no longer had to fend off the slapping, entangling branches. Now it was much easier to concentrate on the seriousness of his mission. Indeed, it had begun to be hard to believe that they would ever catch up to anybody, flailing as they had been through all that dense bush.

This was certainly much better, and Shaw was again able to present the dignified figure that befitted a member of the Force on the lonely trail into the hinterland. Although he was growing a little tender where he sat, and the insides of his thighs and calves were abrading against the serge of his trousers, he took the trouble to continue to sit tall and erect in the saddle.

The two-dollar rancher had despaired of making the tracks problem come out right. So he had decided to head down that particular trail on which, if he had been pursuing anyone at all, he'd have preferred the anyone to take flight.

Then, to his considerable relief, he discovered that his companion never looked down at the trail anyway to see if they were following tracks or not. In fact, the man had the most unusual way of riding with his back stretched straight up like a jack pine pole and his neck and head tilted higher still on top of it.

And with that minor problem out of the way, the two-dollar rancher began to address his mind again to other, more pressing realities, although he now did this with a growing apprehension that nothing devised by him had a snowball's chance in hell of coming to a useful result.

Yet he was compelled to try; and the thought that hammered most insistently against his beleaguered brain was that he had better be back in the settlement before Sergeant Petersen, that when he got there he had better get hold of his unpredictable friend and ensure the results that at the moment he could only hope for with little faith—specifically, get Little Boy the hell out of his cellar and into Big Meadow's cabin to await the police—and finally that he'd have to leave Shaw behind someplace in the meantime in order to attend to these things.

So he set a hard and steady pace.

He rode some twenty miles or more westward on the trail he had chosen. He then cut over a steep ridge to the north, angling up a long, sloping sidehill on one side and straight down a precipitous slope on the other, feet braced forward in the stirrups against the jolting of the awkward downhill gait.

He cut through three swamp meadows, where the horses bogged to their bellies and lunged in panic toward higher ground just before giving up altogether.

For nearly two hours he followed a wide stream, wading the horses across it half a dozen times in water so deep that there was no way that a rider could keep his feet out of it.

Then he struck directly through the bush with even more abandon than had been the case earlier when he had been at least pretending to look for track. By the time he found a trail again that he cared to use, it was too late and dark to make a proper camp.

So he hobbled the horses while he cooked the first grub of the day—noon had been ignored completely—then tethered the animals for the night. Then he spread out a tarpaulin and some bedding on top of it, noting with satisfaction that Shaw could hardly walk, and that when he did so it was with spread legs reminiscent of a child carrying an accident in his trousers. Gyp did not comment on this. He merely grunted that he didn't reckon it would rain, but even if it did, there wasn't time to make it worthwhile putting the tent up, and called it a day.

The two-dollar rancher was wrong because it did rain—and on account of it he broke that camp at dawn on a hurried breakfast of coffee and pancakes and rode through the morning, wet and silent and hunched in the saddle in that resignation to weather of men who must endure because they cannot avoid.

When in early afternoon the sun broke out from the weakening overcast, he stopped on a south-facing slope. There he and his sodden trail companion dried themselves and ate deer meat jerky while the horses grazed on long tethers, and the steam rose from the edges of the saddle blankets.

His satisfaction increased as he discovered that the Royal Canadian Mounted Police could barely stand, let alone walk.

He need only get Shaw into the saddle just once more. He soon did that, and he pressed on again until early in the evening, when he brought them up at an old cabin and barn beyond a convergence of several trails.

There he broke into the pack to make a hot and enormous meal for them both, after which he brought in Shaw's bedding but not his own, and all of the grub that was left in the pack.

Then, in the first words of explanation he had offered for anything since their departure the day before, he declared his intention: "I'm going to leave you here while I scout around. I can't quite figure which way Little Boy must have gone. I'll be back in a couple of days. You've got enough grub, and I'll leave your horse in the big corral by the barn. The feed in there'll keep him for a week. Just whatever the hell you do, don't go anywhere."

It was, of course, a monumental lie, but lies were coming easier all the time. Gyp left forthwith after delivering it, and since he'd brought them in a huge rambling circle back to within an hour of Big Meadow, he rode light-heartedly in anticipation of straightening up the whole absurd mess in what was left of the day. His determination to deal like iron with Big Meadow Charlie had grown so resolute that he anticipated no other result.

He'd thought, too, that he was getting back in plenty of time before Petersen, a whole day ahead by the most stringent interpretation of Petersen's stated three or four days.

It was, therefore, bloody bad news, on stopping first at his own place to turn loose the pack mare and, while he was at it perhaps, to check the contents of his root cellar, to find Sergeant Petersen looking a whole lot too damned much at home, right in his own cabin.

X

Petersen occupied the big chair, the one that belonged to Big Meadow Charlie and in which Big Meadow did his serious sitting and saying nothing for hours on end, and Gyp wished fervently that Big Meadow could be there right now and not Petersen. Apart from anything else there was a certain comfort in Big Meadow Charlie, a warmth that emanated from the generous hugeness of him, which you never find in the disciplined leanness of men like Petersen.

But wishing would not make Big Meadow suddenly appear, any more than it could take them all back in time to before this awkward business had happened, nor forward to when it would all be over, though Gyp dreaded to think what would be the shape of things then.

Anyway, Petersen obviously wished some things himself, and mainly he wished to know about a lot of matters that

Gyp did know about but wished he didn't know about, or had never known about and, if having to know about, would never have to discuss.

About the only thing at the moment, in fact, that Gyp really wanted to know about was one thing he didn't; but when he considered taking a bucket into the cellar on the pretext of fetching some potatoes to find it out, he realized that he did not possess that kind of guts. And anyway, he thought it probably better if Petersen did not, now or at any time in the future, know that there was a trap door underneath that bear hide.

Apart from all of this, Petersen began hitting him with questions so persistently that about all he had time to do on his own behalf was convey his sinking feeling with himself wrapped around it to his bunk, where he sat on the edge and lay back on his elbows.

"Where is Shaw?"

A nice, neat question, that. Where is Shaw? An hour's ride from here, waiting for me while I go see which way Little Boy went. Where is Shaw? In pain where he sits, unaware of lies, in a special bliss of his own making.

"I had to leave him behind. Mainly, I had to leave his behind behind. He got a bad case of saddle sores. I left him in an old cabin with some grub. I'll fetch him when his lumps get better."

Petersen was icy. "You left here yesterday morning and you've come back tonight, and you mean to tell me that in that short time you got Shaw's hind end so raw you couldn't bring him back?"

"He didn't hold up so good."

"Neither does your story. What were you doing out there anyway?"

"Shaw wanted to look for Little Boy."

"*I know* that. I *told* you not to let Shaw make some cockeyed adventure out of this stupid business. What possible sense could it make to go out and ride around in the bush for two days?"

Indeed, what could it? Not much, when having got an easy policeman with whom you had that standing arrangement to play games out of the way, you come back to find yourself at the night before yesterday—but this time it is a different policeman, and he is like horseshoe nails driving into the quick of your guilt.

Gyp said: "He's your boy, not mine."

"Where is Little Boy?"

"Now, how the hell would I know that?"

"I didn't ask you how you'd know it. I asked you where he is."

"To tell you the sure enough truth, right as of this minute, I do not know—and that is a fact."

Which was a sort of technical truth, even though in its fundamental nature a lie, and Gyp clung a little desperately to that fact; and the desperation was not because his conscience was much bothered by some kinds of lying, of which this kind was one, but because he had a strong feeling that to tell a lie to Petersen was certain, in the final result, to be dangerous. Petersen had that competent efficiency about him that made you, as soon as you had uttered your lie, hear Petersen repeating it to a judge as one of many assembled measures of your sins.

Petersen, clearly, did not know about that minimal honor between men that rules out questions to which a man will be forced to lie, and Gyp, though it was growing quite dark in the cabin, made no move to light the lamp. He no longer wished to look at Petersen, and darkness was more comfortable than finding other directions for his eyes.

The next question landed. "You're involved with Annie Charlie, aren't you?"

Gyp had not expected it to come so directly, and yet an unease that warned him that something unwanted was going to happen had told him that this would come up, even if for no more reason than that men like Petersen always have to pass judgment on men like himself.

He dealt with it. "If it doesn't rain tomorrow," he declared, "it ought to be a nice day."

"And your being involved with Annie Charlie," Petersen persisted, "makes you just damned well certain to know a lot more than you're letting on. If I'd realized it sooner I wouldn't have left Shaw here alone for you to sidetrack him."

"In fact," Gyp said, "if it would hold for a few days, I'd start cutting my hay."

"There's no use your denying it, either," Petersen added. "This cabin wouldn't be nearly so clean as it is if you didn't have a woman here at least part of the time. There are three hairpins over there on top of that old trunk in the corner, and I saw Annie coming away from here today on my way up from the village."

"It sure would be nice to start haying. If some people would just mind their own business and let me mind mine, I would put my mower into the cut first thing tomorrow morning. You ever mow hay? It is sure as hell a nice job. It is something you do all by yourself, just you and your horses, and . . ."

"Sandhouse, you bastard!" Petersen exploded. "I don't give a damn about your blasted hay! Now you listen to me, and you start talking sense."

"I believe that."

"Believe what?"

"That you don't give a damn about my hay."

"Oh, God," Petersen moaned, despair coming into his voice with the anger. "I don't care about your hay, and I would be glad to let you mow the stuff and whatever else you have to do with it. But I have some unfinished business to do here, and you are not helping me one damned bit—which would be all right, except that it happens to be very important business. There is a body in the morgue in Williams Lake. That always makes it an important business, even as important as your hay, believe it or not.

"And don't get me wrong about Annie. What you do with her is your business, although I can't see why men like you don't either leave the Indian women alone, or marry one properly if you can't. But it only matters to me because Annie just happens to be Little Boy's sister and Big Meadow Charlie's daughter, which means, Sandhouse," and the persistent, authoritarian clarity came back to Petersen's voice to hammer out the remaining words, carefully spaced, "that you cannot be as ignorant of things around here as you're trying to make out."

Or as I would like to be, Gyp reflected, but he kept it to himself.

There was a silence then as the two men sat together in the darkness and Gyp strained with his ears to pick up some sounds from below that might confirm for him what he wished were not the case. It was a strange kind of listening, straining for sounds that he hoped, as hard as he listened for them, wouldn't be there. And if they weren't, would that tell him that Little Boy was gone, or that Little Boy knew how to keep very quiet? You could lie awake a whole night on such a question, and Gyp realized that he was probably about to do just that.

Petersen spoke again: "Sandhouse, there can be a very serious penalty for helping someone avoid arrest. It carries half the maximum of the offense committed by the fugitive himself, and when you consider that the offense in this case has resulted in a body in a morgue, and when you consider the view the judge will take of the kind of obstructing that I believe is going on around here, surely you realize that you are not dabbling in something that will only have you kept in after school for an hour."

What Gyp realized as well was that the view the judge would take was going to be so competently nurtured by Petersen that no explanation Gyp possibly could give could do anything but make it worse. In the recesses of his apprehensions he already had tried, and it was like the cat trying to explain the dead canary.

And Petersen waited for it all to sink in. But he needn't have, for something quite close to what he had just said had been sinking into Gyp's reluctant consciousness since at least the point at which Little Boy had taken shape out of the shadows in the potato bin, if not considerably before.

Petersen went on: "Now let us take as generous a view as we can. Let us suppose that you *don't* know where Little Boy is. But it's a damned certain thing that Big Meadow Charlie knows, and Annie, too, for that matter.

"So if you really have their best interests at heart—after all Big Meadow is almost your father-in-law, so to speak—why don't you see if you can get them to realize the seriousness of helping Little Boy avoid arrest? Then maybe take it a step farther and see if they won't tip you off to where he's holed up?"

Gyp got up then and stomped across the floor on his saddle-weary legs to light the lamp that stood on the table under the window. He lit it slowly, turning the wick up to a moderate flame and blowing the match out afterward with great deliberation. It all gave him time to think, whatever good that might do him.

After all, wasn't that what he needed, a chance to talk sense into Big Meadow Charlie? And yet there was something in the proposition that so offended him, though he couldn't quite put his finger on it, that he knew he wasn't going to be able to do it. Talk to Big Meadow, yes, but on that pretext, never.

"Let me tell you something, Petersen. Big Meadow is my friend. I don't concern myself with what he does, but I cannot help the fact that some of what he does comes to my attention. That is unavoidable in a big place like this, where Big Meadow and I happen to live. But that doesn't mean that anything he does is any of my damned business. I do not, as a matter of fact, think that everything he does that I happen to know about makes sense, or is the best thing for himself, or for anyone else, for that matter, that he could do. But Big Meadow Charlie is my friend, and what he does is not, therefore, any of my business whatsoever, at all, in any way, shape, or form. If some of what he does happens to get in the way of what I'm trying to do myself, I will deal with that part of it, but not one forkful more. So you go tell your own things to Big Meadow Charlie, and leave me the hell out of it."

Petersen exploded. "Sandhouse, you're a fool! But that's not all you are. You are also a lousy liar. Well, let me spell it out for you, so even you can get it through your thick head. Little Boy Charlie killed a man. I know Crease was a bad bastard, but at this point that makes no difference. I don't expect Big Meadow Charlie to realize that necessarily, and I can understand him trying to keep Little Boy under wraps. But there is no excuse for you, Gyp Sandhouse, and if I find one straw of evidence that you know where Little Boy is, I will see you in jail for the count as surely as if you were hiding him under your own damned bed. Have you got that?"

"I got a horse tied up that needs letting loose. That is all I got right now, outside of a desire to get some sleep—which, after I let that horse loose, I'm going to proceed with straight away. You can stay up all night and ask questions about Little Boy and Big Meadow, but you will have to make up your own answers. Me, I'm done with it until at least tomorrow morning."

Gyp rose to go, and Petersen stood up as well. "I'll go with you to let the horse loose."

"That is very kind of you, but it's not exactly a two-man job, letting a horse loose, especially this horse, who is very gentle and does not mind at all being let loose."

"Don't be an ass. I'm going with you. If you want me to be crude and say I don't trust you, that's how it is. I don't trust you."

"You will get a star for honesty and you can move to the front of the row. Don't trip in the dark. I don't intend to light a lantern for an expedition as limited as this one."

Gyp stripped the saddle and the blanket from the old horse. The gelding rolled in the yard, then made his way to the creek for water. Gyp and Petersen made their own way back to the cabin, and as if to let Gyp know he acceded to the truce for the night, Petersen spoke of mundane things. "You've got rats under this cabin."

And Gyp grasped wildly at the meaning of that for, in fact, he'd never let a rat get near the cabin, and least of all the root cellar, and so it was a matter for instant calculation why Petersen thought so, and what Gyp had better have to say of it.

He tried, nonchalantly: "Yeh. I got rats. Biggest rats you ever saw."

"I can believe it. I heard one this evening before you came in. Prowling around under the floor."

"Kind of a thumping sound? Like bumping into things?" It was like the make-believe with Shaw, you had to get into the mood of the thing or it wouldn't come off.

"Yes, that describes it."

"That's him all right. Been trying to catch him for a hell of a while. Smartest rat you ever saw. Must be the size of a small dog. Granddaddy of the pack. Makes a hole like a coyote where he goes." Gyp rather liked adding that bit about the hole. It had the sort of realism that made his prevarications professional.

Peterson said, enthusiastically: "I'd like to see that."

"Well, hell, you never see 'im."

"No, I mean the hole where he goes in."

"Oh, well. You know, it's just a hole. Seen one hole, seen 'em all."

"Well, still I'd like to see it."

"In the morning."

"Oh, sure. No hurry."

Gyp did not go as straight away to sleep as he had declared he would, but then he had hardly expected to either.

Instead he ranged over the mess he'd got into back where he should have exploded with astonishment at Little Boy's presence in the potato bin and been done with it right there. It was even grinding to realize that Big Meadow had so surely known him that the ploy had worked.

But now the task of so arranging events as to unravel it all defeated him, even in the thinking. He had somehow to get Petersen the devil out of the way—and that wouldn't be the simple matter it had been with Shaw—then get Big Meadow to relocate Little Boy. After all that he would have to persuade Big Meadow to unwrap Little Boy for Petersen's benefit from some unsuspicious direction, which of course meant getting Petersen back in the way at an appropriate time after having got him out of the way.

And all of this had somehow to be staged without seeming to be staged, *especially* without seeming to be staged by Gyp Sandhouse.

Gyp did sleep a little in the early hours of the morning, but it was the kind of sleep you couldn't be sure you'd had or that would do you any good anyway, and it was invaded constantly by a profound disquiet about this business of the rat hole. At one point Gyp was digging an appropriate tunnel with his fingernails grown long for the purpose so that he would have something fit for demonstration in the morning, and at another he kept crawling back and forth with Petersen in skeptical pursuit, and Big Meadow Charlie laughing himself silly from the top log on the corral.

But by morning Gyp had a plan.

He was going to bolt. There was nothing else for it. He completely despaired of rearranging events to give himself the least semblance of innocence, and he was fed up to the back teeth with the whole affair. It wasn't his business, he'd got sucked into it against his will, and he saw no reason to stay anywhere near it, especially now that there was no way to come out clean.

He wasn't at all sure how he would emerge again in some far place without more trouble with the police, but he would have to deal with that later. For the time being he could only deal with the getting out—and that he would accomplish quite simply.

He would pack up the old mare again, with a whacking good outfit, then head off with the declared intention of going to get Little Boy, come hell or high water. He'd bluff it through, even with such a skeptic as Petersen, and once he was out of sight they could look for him forever. Finding Little Boy would be a paper trail treasure hunt at a kid's birthday party by comparison.

And Big Meadow Charlie could buy the place at tax sale the next time around. Or better yet, Gyp would deed it to him, all transactions secretly by mail, and send him as well a bill of sale for the stock.

Gyp would be in some far place with his beard grown long and a new name, and he would not be known.

It was no more far-fetched a scheme than the immediate events in Gyp's life warranted.

XI

It didn't go badly, at least not to start with. Not until Big Meadow and Annie appeared on the scene.

Gyp had risen early and lit a fire and put on a kettle to boil for coffee.

Petersen, who had had the bunk while Gyp had done with a horse blanket on the floor, had wakened with him. But he hadn't followed when Gyp, after setting the water to boil, excused himself and went outside.

Gyp had then caught the saddle horse and the pack mare and fed them both a ration of hay to make up for the skimpiness of the grazing in the big yard around the cabin, then put the saddle on the horse and the pack rig on the mare.

He had returned to the cabin after that to find Petersen up and dressed. Wordlessly he had set about making a breakfast of hotcakes and salt deer meat; he did not even reply when Petersen grunted his appreciation for the boiled coffee that preceded the meal. It seemed just possible that if he avoided conversation, or at any rate made no contributions to it himself, the earliness of the hour might discourage Petersen's talk, and he might be able to get great things done along this new course before he was obliged, again, to begin to account for himself.

They had eaten in silence.

Then, with the breakfast over, Gyp had ignored the debris

on the table, taking instead a large square of canvas that he had spread on the floor. Then he began throwing things onto it, an assortment of possessions and supplies from around the cabin: socks, shirts, moose meat jerky, rice, flour—the bits of this and that which a man might use over a long time on the trail. There was already the tent and some basic gear with the pack boxes at the corral, where he had stripped the mare the evening before on his arrival.

Petersen had watched with interest and finally broken the silence. "What's all this in aid of?"

Gyp then had thrown in the last of what seemed necessary to the intention of never returning under the guise of being gone for a week. Then he gathered the four corners of the canvas in his hands to form a pouch, lifted it, and swung it skillfully to one side, then turned so that it fell on his back with the gathered ends over his shoulder in his grip.

"I'm going out to find Little Boy. And before you get excited over that, you listen while I talk. I'm fed up to the earholes with this damned business, and it's not even my business. I didn't know Moses Crease from a coyote's uncle, and I didn't have anything to do with him getting in the way of however he got killed—although I understand there were some reasons why that wasn't such a bad idea. I have not, either, arranged Little Boy's lodgings since, and I do not feel like I have to do anything to help you find him. I am not even sorry that the police business right now is operating at a loss in this particular matter. And I am fed up with your hard talk in the bargain. So unless you have some good reason that I haven't heard about to keep me from my stated purpose, I'm packing that mare and taking my leave."

It had worked, to Gyp's considerable amazement. Although he had assured himself repeatedly that until Petersen actually had something to arrest him for, there wasn't a damned thing the sergeant could do to stop him, it was nonetheless a hard thing to believe.

But it had worked, for when Gyp had delivered this enormous declaration of his intent, Petersen had merely shrugged and told him to have it his own way, it would all come out the same in the end.

Whereupon Petersen had fetched the last of the coffee and made himself comfortable on the splitting block at the wood pile in front of the cabin. From there he had watched with only a moderate display of interest while Gyp, with the saddle horse and the pack mare both brought conveniently close, had sorted and hefted and stowed in the pack boxes and fetched a few more bits of this and that.

Gyp had the pack boxes slung on the pack saddle with the tent and his clothing and bedroll balanced on top of it all and the beginnings of the hitch thrown to lash everything down, when Big Meadow Charlie and Annie arrived.

That was the point up to which this new plan did not go badly.

In fact it had gone so well, this new course of Gyp's, this bolting out from under, that he had begun to be grateful for how little attachment he had to his worldly goods, his land, and his cattle and his rusty machinery. It was true that he had invested a lot of years in their securing, but they meant nothing in themselves. They were valuable only as a means of avoiding the world, and now that this accident of entangling circumstance had brought the world, or at any rate some of its more disagreeable ingredients, to Upper Meadow, Gyp was confident that he could do just as well in some other piece of bush with a rifle, a few traps, and a gold pan as he had done in this one with horses, cows, and hay.

But it was short-lived, this going well of Gyp's new course. It expired with the arrival of those whose own courses had become inextricably bound with his in such ways that, try as he might, he could not even for long maintain the illusion of control, far less its substance.

Good mornings were not said, they were passed around in inquiring looks of the kind that go between people who wish ardently to know what in hell the others are up to but have not the least intention of letting it on, much less of asking direct questions.

But not long this feigned indifference for Annie. She shared in the initial exchange of inquiring looks, but then her expression changed, and Gyp knew that something, for her, had suddenly gone seriously wrong.

She asked her first question of Petersen. "Where's he going?"

It was a bad sign that she sought what she wanted of Gyp indirectly through a third party. Anger was a quiet thing with Annie, like a snake not making any noise while he bites your leg, and if she could deal through third parties, she always chose it. Gyp had seen her do it in Big Meadow's cabin in that swarm of in-laws, and he was familiar with the process. His stomach turned over, and when it came right side up again it was in a well-tied square knot.

Petersen said, sarcastically: "He's going to look for Little Boy. At least that's what he says, but I stopped believing most of what he says about dark last night."

Annie dismounted and walked up to Gyp until her face wasn't a foot away from his.

Not a soul other than Gyp could hear her words, for she spoke in the searing undertones of fury, more breath than sound: "What the hell are you doing?"

And he started to make the lie to her that he had made to Petersen, but stopped before any words came out; and then he was ashamed of the momentary intent. He tried for a while not to speak at all, but that wouldn't do either.

So finally he said: "I'm pulling out. I can't stand this thing any longer."

"You *bastard!*" Then: "Like hell you're pulling out!"

And Annie ran to the cabin and into it, and the trap door banged like a rifle shot as it fell back on the floor.

It was staggering that Little Boy could move so fast, even under the imperious command of Annie's anger, but he did; for there he was, large as life, out the cabin door and delivered for the taking.

Petersen, having delayed for a moment to try to catch the significance of this flurry of events, hadn't made it halfway from the wood pile to the doorway.

XII

Petersen looked inquiringly at Gyp. "Little Boy?"

"Little Boy," Gyp acknowledged.

"Well, now, isn't that interesting. *You* haven't been arranging Little Boy's lodging, so *you* aren't responsible for anything." The sarcasm dripped, like heavy icing, down the edges of his words. "You didn't know, right as of this minute, where Little Boy was, and that's a fact."

He walked to where Gyp stood by his pack mare with the loose end of the hitch rope dangling in his hands and shut off the sarcasm the way a man closes a gate behind a bad horse, fast and firmly. Then in his own kind of anger, loud and demanding but coldly controlled: "Would you like to explain it now, or after you talk to a lawyer in town?"

There was, oddly, a certain measure of relief in Gyp in this turn of events, and he found he no longer really gave a damn whether he explained himself to Petersen or not. And that was logical too, he thought, for it was one of life's certainties that Petersen wouldn't believe him even if he now told the truth in all its encumbering exactness.

So he didn't bother, not with the exactness.

He just said: "That surprised me as much as it did you, Petersen. Do you know how to make this hitch on the other side of this horse, by any chance?"

"No, I don't. And I'm not interested."

"Well, I am. So excuse me for a moment. Little Boy, you go over and haul down on this rope and pass it back to me." Then, back to Petersen: "I still have to fetch Shaw."

"But you don't need all that outfit to go fetch Shaw."

"True. But I'm not going to change it all now."

And I'm going to make a damned long day of it both going and coming, for everybody's benefit, he added to himself. The disclosure of Little Boy and where he had been staying had robbed Gyp's plan to bolt of what little point there had been in it. It now seemed that he must pin his hopes on what chance there was that he might explain Little Boy's presence in his cellar in terms that would leave him only marginally implicated. But there was no use confessing that Shaw was only an hour's ride out, and that he could have as easily made him endure another hour in the saddle as leave him behind.

The necessity to be seen as innocent in the lodging of Little Boy in his cellar would not necessarily, Gyp decided, be best served by admitting to his prevarications in the matter of Shaw's whereabouts.

Little Boy had passed the rope through what would have to do for the prescribed twists and loops on the other side of the pack mare and passed the remainder of it back over the top.

Gyp took it and cinched down then and held the end tight before tying while he went on with his conversation with Petersen.

"I do not, myself, make a diamond hitch, and neither does

Little Boy. Little Boy has trouble even tying his laces. But whatever I end up with on the other side of this pack horse will do me today. Now I'm going to tell you something, and I don't give a damn whether you believe it or not. But it happens to be a fact that I did not agree to, arrange for, permit, or otherwise have knowledge of Little Boy being stashed in my cellar."

"Oh, I'm so impressed with that. It has the same ring of truth about it as your story about the rat. The one as big as a small dog."

"Yeah. Well, that wasn't so convincing, I will admit. But just as of this moment, I am only talking about the time when Little Boy was actually stashed in the cellar. That was an event about which I was, and I am still, in complete innocence. Does that help?"

"Let us take the generous view, Sandhouse. Let us suppose that you are telling the truth and that Little Boy was stashed in your cellar absolutely without your knowledge. It is inconceivable, of course, but let us suppose it. The answer is no, it does not help you, not one small bit. It does not help you because your innocence is so muddied by subsequent events."

"You're a hard man, Petersen. But let us do a little more supposing. Let us suppose that I am still telling you the truth when I tell you that finding Little Boy was in my cellar happened in such a haywire way that I never got the chance to fix it so it would look like I never had anything to do with it. Even if I did my damnedest ever since to fix everything to sort of come out right in a way that would leave me unsaddled with this damned thing, which was never any part my scheme, unsaddled with this damned thing just like I'd had nothing to do with the stashing, well, hell, it just never worked out, that's all. Plain bloody bad luck all the way."

And Gyp wondered what it was he'd said there, it had all got so involved in the saying. But it was soon forgotten; for

Little Boy (for the first time, as far as Gyp Sandhouse could ever determine) took matters into his own hands.

While Gyp and Petersen on one side of the old pack mare were engrossed in this game of supposing all kinds of unlikely and complicated things, Little Boy's eyes fell on the saddled horse not ten feet away. His eyes also fell on the open gate where Big Meadow and Annie had come in and not closed up behind them, since they had seen that Gyp had only two horses in at the time and both of them in hand in front of the cabin. Little Boy saw the saddled horse and the open gate and the short space of ten feet that separated him from the horse, and he managed to put these with the fact that everyone's attention was fixed on what was being said on the other side of the pack mare. And in the sort of unthought coalescence of evident things immediately to hand and never any more, which provided a basis for everything Little Boy did, he stepped over to the horse, unslipped the bridle reins from the stump they were wrapped on, climbed aboard, and left.

That was where Gyp's last piece of supposing got lost, and he and Petersen just never did get back to it.

XIII

Petersen suffered, visibly.

Gyp could see by so much about the man—the neatness of his dress, the briskness of his step, the businesslike, no-nonsense approach to his work—that he was wholly accustomed to having charge of people and events in situations that were orderly by application of his own will, if nothing else.

This chaos was too much, Gyp could see that, and so he said, very quietly: "What would you like to do next?"

And Petersen stared at him as if unable to decide whether to destroy him in a rage of anger and frustration, or to treat him like an incomprehensible idiot, tolerable only because nothing of any useful consequence could be expected of him anyway.

Finally he said, very quietly: "Get Little Boy. I want to get Little Boy without any more stupid games."

"I didn't arrange that last bit, you know," Gyp said, in defense against this latest reference to his culpability.

"I could believe you. I could believe you because it would require intelligence to arrange something as deft as that, and I do not credit you with intelligence. On the other hand, you are a liar and you would like to have arranged it even if you didn't, so I'm holding you responsible for it anyway. Would you like to hear how I'll tell it to the judge?"

"No."

"Then do something about some horses—because this time you're going to find Little Boy and I'm going to be there with you."

"That'll take some time. I'll have to strip this pack mare and go find what little saddle stock I have left, which will take me anywhere from a couple of hours to a couple of days, depending on how far from home my cayuses are looking for grass these days. And I have to go to the village to borrow a couple of saddles because both mine are in use elsewhere, as you know. If the demand holds up, I'm going into the riding club business."

Petersen, given this summary of their transport situation, turned his attention to Annie and Big Meadow. For they, as Gyp himself recognized at that same moment, had two saddled horses in their possession, and while Gyp wouldn't have the brass to ask them for their mounts, he assumed that Petersen would have the authority to requisition them, and wouldn't hesitate to do so.

But Annie and Big Meadow must have had plans of their own for their horses, for Annie had remounted—Big Meadow had never dismounted, since that was quite a task for him and in all this disarray so far there had been no reason to undertake it—and though they had lingered on the edges of the scene while the two white men had bandied words about, they were ready to leave at any moment, and they now did so.

Gyp watched them go, then looked at Petersen and shrugged. "It was an idea. But it's just as well it didn't work."

"What makes you say that?"

"Because," Gyp went on, explaining the new reality to Petersen pretty much at the same time that it was becoming evident to himself, "they're going to need those horses, and a little time as well. They're going to have to catch up to Little Boy before we do, to take care of him. Otherwise we wouldn't catch up to him at all. Not while there'd be anything left to catch up to."

"Explain that."

"Little Boy is kind of helpless, I guess. He'll be scared panicky out there by himself anyway, and if we got anywhere near him he'd run that horse in the bush and probably kill himself."

"You told me he was harmless. You didn't say he was help-less as well."

Gyp thought a long while, because he was back to the fundamental puzzle that defied any explanation: How could Little Boy have done the killing—a killing that called for such enormous resolve that the other men couldn't do it, even pressed by fear for their lives?

But the puzzle stuck, and Gyp passed it by. He tried to explain about Little Boy: "I guess you'd call him useless, only . . ." And Gyp stuck there for a while, because he'd never stopped to consider why you wouldn't call him useless; he only knew you wouldn't, and he couldn't figure it out—he only knew that he couldn't put that term on Little Boy without feeling mean and guilty inside himself.

So he tried a different way. "People have to take care of him, that's all. He can't take care of himself. Can't do the simplest damned things, and if he spent a night alone in the bush he'd probably be dead of fright by morning. He's got to be someplace he feels safe, or he's got to have someone with him."

Gyp was done, and a silence followed in which Gyp began unlashing the pack in order to strip it from the mare so he could ride her bareback to fetch his remaining horses.

Petersen spoke to him once more; and to listen the better, Gyp paused in his work.

"I don't know if what you have just told me makes any more sense of what has been going on here or not. It certainly can't make any less. But I can tell you that if what you have been doing has been your idea of how to help Little Boy, you sure as hell have some misguided ideas. And it does not reduce one damned particle the mess you have made for yourself, which you are going to explain to a judge when this is all over, regardless of what else happens. If you have a shred of sense, don't make it any worse."

Gyp went back to undoing the pack and stripping the mare. He had a sense of resignation, an acceptance of the fact that events were indifferent to the well-being of Gyp Sandhouse. It wasn't that he had any great desire to control events, either. He just wished they weren't so hell bent on pushing him around.

XIV

As it happened, Gyp's remaining horseflesh was not all that far out of Upper Meadow, and by noon he had it rounded up and had borrowed a couple of badly worn saddles of a very ancient vintage from the village.

Petersen and he then had a last meal in the convenience of the cabin. After that Gyp repacked the mare—he reduced the load by taking out those items that had been surreptitiously added in preparation for an indefinite journey, making it more suited to the few days at most that they would now be out— and they set off.

It was an easy matter to find the tracks of Little Boy's shod saddle horse on the trail westward, and no surprise either when they were soon joined by the tracks of two more horses. And it wasn't hard to estimate that Big Meadow and Annie, traveling lightly with no more outfit than they could tie behind their saddles, had gone by there while Gyp was still fetching his horses.

But it was not so easy for Gyp to come to some accommodation with his new role in this bizarre drama, and his desperation, which had ebbed in a kind of fatalistic relief on the releasing of Little Boy, had begun to rise again.

For he could not chase down and turn in Little Boy. He knew that ultimately, for everyone's sake, the turning in of Little Boy, however accomplished, was the only course; but he knew that he could not be the one to do it.

As the desperation rose, so also did the urge, again, to bolt. And this time, handily, it did not need for its fulfillment any more outfit than Gyp could tie behind his saddle.

Gyp acknowledged this urge, this compulsion to run to some distant anonymity, and he nurtured it a while in his mind, passing it about from one side to the other while he savored what it promised.

What it promised was not being stuck with the turning in of Little Boy, and the promise tasted very good.

Gyp put the urge away then, for the moment.

And as he did that, he comforted himself with a further notion (which for all he knew might have been sheer self-deception, but he was prepared to entertain it anyway), that if he were in some far place when Little Boy was finally taken into custody, his part in the preceding difficulties would not seem nearly so necessary of prosecution as they would if he were still standing handily by, where Sergeant Petersen could have him for the picking up.

Gyp pressed on through the afternoon at the modest pace his lesser-grade horses could stand, and when the sun was hitting the pine tops at the long angle of early evening, he sought out water and made camp.

When he'd done the necessary things—hobbled out the horses, pitched the tent, made the grub, and cleaned up afterward, then tethered the horses against the chance of their traveling too far on the hobbles once their bellies were full of grass—he took his bedroll and said the first thing he'd said to Petersen since they had set off.

"I'm going to sleep out tonight. You take the tent. If it rains, I'll join you. Don't be offended. It's just that I like fresh air. It's what keeps me young. G'night."

Whereupon he settled beneath a spreading spruce tree for the night some distance off from the camp; and just for a while again before he slept, he let the bolting urge come out again, and he talked with it.

He spoke of a far valley in the Selkirks, five hundred miles by the route you'd have to take, to the southeast, where he once had hunted elk with his father and where you could always get colors in a gold pan, and just once in a long while poor wages for a few yards of creek bottom. There was an ancient cabin there, and if the winter snows had not been too hard on it, a man could quickly make it livable.

Gyp traced in his mind the long route through cattle country and homestead valleys that would get him there, the way of the back trail and the little-used road, the way that would avoid the highways and towns and come to thoroughfares only for the river crossings, the way that would let a man disappear into the bush at the sound of an approaching motor. He thought of the places where he would kill a deer and dry the meat to keep himself along the way.

When he had put the bolting urge back in its lair before he went to sleep, he had agreed to arrange the means of his departure.

XV

All through the next day, Gyp preserved his silence with Petersen, even when it became clear to him that Big Meadow Charlie, having caught up to Little Boy, had done the same thing as he had done earlier with Shaw: come in a huge circle back toward Big Meadow.

And there was no longer much evident need to keep things such as where they all were a secret; but for the sake of his intent to comply with the bolting urge, the detailed plans for which were still vague, Gyp opted for what came naturally to him anyway—a closed mouth.

So Gyp did not break silence when he realized with some amusement that Big Meadow Charlie had in fact drawn all the participants in this bizarre business into close reach of each other—probably not more than an hour's ride from one camp to the next, including the cabin where Shaw was cached—and all of these within an hour of Big Meadow itself.

Toward the end of the day the tracks on the trail ahead became visibly fresher. Once where manure had fallen it was bright with the freshness of having been dropped within the hour.

Gyp made camp early so that he would have two or three hours of daylight to himself afterward.

He hobbled the horses out as usual, then set the tent and cooked the meal of dried meat and fried bannock and rolled Petersen's bedding out so Petersen could rest his weary body while he ate. Then he did the cleaning up, as always, while Petersen (as Gyp knew he must) settled into the welcome inertia of the physically exhausted man who, once stretched out, cannot bring himself to move again till morning. Riding is just the kind of work to lay a man out like that when he does a hard day and a half of it for virtually the first time in his life.

Then Gyp tethered the pack mare and Petersen's mount; but he put the saddle back on his own, and tied his bedroll with some extra clothing in it behind the saddle. Petersen, lying weary in the tent, was not even aware of these things. So Gyp had him quite by surprise when, his horse in lead, he came by the tent to declare himself, to be believed or not as Petersen might choose.

"I'm going ahead to scout track. I think I can maybe locate Big Meadow's camp. You'll have to wait here. And whatever the hell you do, don't go anywhere."

If that bothered Petersen, he didn't show it. He only looked back with a steady gaze that said, if anything, that he knew Gyp had him down at this moment, but that this had nothing to do with how things would turn out in the end. In the end, Petersen would be wholly and totally on top, in charge, calling the shots one, two, three, and this moment of disadvantage would be of no consequence.

He said: "Sandhouse."

"Yes."

"Use your head."

And Gyp did not acknowledge that at all; he only mounted up and left. For the second time he had cached a policeman in the bush. At the rate he was going, he reflected, he could lose the whole Williams Lake detachment in three weeks.

It was then he discovered that it was one thing to have made this final and irrevocable resolve to bolt, but quite another to be sure how to accomplish it. Having ridden out of the camp he'd made just so that he could leave Petersen behind, he realized that his next move was far from clear.

It was clear enough that Little Boy had to be turned over to Petersen. It was clear enough that, as of this moment, the responsibility for that, by a tortuous route that Gyp's mind did not care even to attempt to unravel, lay in Gyp's hands, and that was a fact.

It was clear enough too to Gyp Sandhouse that he had no intention whatsoever of actually trying to do that necessary thing. For, as surely as the winters of his life outnumbered the summers, he couldn't do it for reasons he did not wish to discuss with himself—and even if he did try to do just that simple thing, the attempt would turn into another round of sinister implication for himself.

But having resolved not to have anything to do with this responsibility (a responsibility that should never have been his but now unquestionably was, by this strange process he would not let his mind inspect), he found that he could not face Big Meadow and Little Boy.

He did not let his mind inspect that, either.

But his mind was obliged, against his will, to inspect the fact that if he could not deal with this responsibility about

Little Boy, he had then to turn it over to someone else. And of course the someone else was Annie—who would also do, quite incidentally, as the necessary someone else to rescue Shaw, whose location he would make known, along with Petersen's, in his unburdening.

And so he narrowed his attention to this one problem: how to talk to Annie without seeing Big Meadow and Little Boy. It would not be easy. They would all three be in camp together, and cutting her out by herself without the others being aware looked largely impossible.

Along the trail the fresh tracks hardly needed more than the most occasional and indifferent glance from Gyp to tell him that the camp he sought could not be as much as an hour away. Meanwhile, Gyp's progress was as erratic as the comings and goings of impossibilities in his head. He would ride sometimes quickly, sometimes slowly; often he would stop altogether and lean forward with his hands taking his weight on the pommel of the saddle while his mind would go around in another of its ill-directed circles. And then, as if to reflect the completeness of his muddle, the confusion and the indecision that had hold of him, he turned right around on the trail and began riding in the opposite direction.

And there, her horse reined up on the trail from where she had been watching these unusual movements, these stoppings and startings and the final turning about in his confusion, was Annie.

When he stopped beside her and managed to meet her eyes, he found that she was looking at him in a most penetrating and measuring way.

XVI

For a while they did not speak; and in that while Gyp looked for the words that would fit the uncomfortable things he had to say, but he did not find any.

Finally he asked: "How far is your camp?"

She said: "Half hour."

There was more silence and more of that measuring gaze from Annie, and under it Gyp did not like himself.

The not liking himself created its own kind of pressure, and suddenly Gyp plunged into what had to be said. "Big Meadow's got to turn him in. You have to make him understand that."

Annie said, evenly and firmly: "*You* have to make him understand that."

"No. Not me. Not any more. I tried once and it didn't work."

"You didn't try. You wouldn't listen. You only shut him up. He needed time. You can do it now."

"I am not going to see him again, so you have to do it."

Gyp watched for what that would mean to Annie, but she was collected now, and she was not revealing herself the way she had when she'd been taken by surprise at the cabin at Upper Meadow.

She persisted. "You got to tell him. You got to make him understand."

He persisted. "No. You can do it. I'm not going to do it, so you have to do it." And then in a burst of harshness born of his determination he said, "I'm getting out. I can't take it, and I'm leaving. I can't stand the old man's trouble. I will give him the meadow and even the cattle, but I can't stand his trouble."

"You can't buy away his trouble. His heart is askin' for Little Boy, not for meadow and cattle."

Gyp's eyes fell away from her face, and he stared downward to the ground. He forced more words out. "Look, it's just this simple: He's got to turn Little Boy in, and Petersen's only an hour up this trail. If the old man tells Little Boy it's all right, Little Boy won't be afraid."

She cut him off. "We know that. It's later in jail Little Boy will die from being away from his people."

Gyp's reply was impatient from his own desperation. "You could explain that to the judge. Maybe he'd understand."

"Nobody knows Little Boy 'cept his own people. Nobody's going to believe it."

"I can't help that."

"The old man needs you."

"All the old man needs right now is for one of us to tell him to do what he has to do. And you can do that just as well as I can. And you will have to do that because I'm leaving. I'm going to turn my horse off this trail and disappear into the bush, and when I come out again I will be so far from here nobody will know me or give a damn, and by then it will all be finished with."

"If you leave, I leave."

Gyp looked at her again, and it was not hard to say what he had to say then, because he did not like himself in that moment even one small measure. He said: "You're not going with me because I'm a no-good bastard, and it's time you quit wasting your life on me."

She said: "I didn't say I was going with you. I just said if you leave, I leave." Then in further explanation: "I'll ride where you do, so you'll know the old man is alone. But that's all."

"You wouldn't."

"Try me."

In defiance, Gyp turned his horse off the trail and plunged into the timber at a fast trot.

Annie followed, and she was never more than two lengths behind him.

He chose the toughest thickets he could find, and she was all but there to meet him as he came out on the far side.

His horse lathered, and finally he had to rein up to wind him; and when he did, Annie stopped beside him. He looked at her to puzzle out, if he could, how in hell you could be so absolutely run ragged by this little wisp of a woman, and she smiled at him with the cool sweetness of spring water on a hot day.

And he asked her: "How could you leave the old man alone in his trouble?"

She asked him: "How could you?"

And he exploded: "But, dammit, he's your dad and Little Boy's your brother! They *belong* to *you!*"

"They belong to you, too."

"No."

But it was lamely said, and she said no more.

Finally he said: "Let's go."

And they rode together back to pick up the trail and make their way to Big Meadow's camp.

XVII

Within the hour, easily, they rode into the camp to find Big Meadow and Little Boy taking their ease before a small fire set in front of a canvas leanto that gave just enough rudimentary shelter for three bedrolls.

Gyp took his own horse and Annie's as well and stripped

them and set them both on hobbles, then stowed the saddles and blankets and bridles under a tree where the rest of Big Meadow's gear, and Gyp's own saddle, were cached.

By the time he came into the warmth and the light that the fire was making against the gathering dusk, Annie had boiled a billy and made tea.

While Gyp sipped he said nothing and allowed himself, again, the considerable pleasure of thinking nothing. It was a much-needed relief after all that taxing work to which he had recently been putting his brain and, in the result, for what?

For what, indeed. It is better, Gyp thought, to do what the moment asks and then wait for events to reveal themselves, than to sweat your head to order them, in the hope that you will be able to predict your tomorrows.

And the silence was so pleasant. It was totally different from the silence with Petersen. With Petersen you had to work at keeping quiet, and even thinking was hard to avoid.

With Big Meadow you were safe and you could come on things in your own good time.

Then at last, the tea finished, Gyp sat up, cross-legged before the fire, his hands resting on the worn tops of his riding boots.

"Big Meadow."

His friend looked up to acknowledge the address and waited for the question.

"Big Meadow, there is this one thing you have to tell me. You have to tell it to me very carefully before we go any farther. I have to know this one thing before I can tell you what we have to do next."

Big Meadow said nothing; but in the saying nothing was the simple assertion that of course he would, for he had never told Gyp any less than Gyp ever asked and always, of course, the truth. And the realization of this simple message in the silence from Big Meadow made Gyp feel guilty, but he did not mind that, for of course Big Meadow did not intend such a thing. Only men like Petersen, white men like Petersen, would intend such a thing, and they would have used words to ensure it.

So Gyp put it to him. "You have to tell me exactly how it was that Moses Crease got killed."

Now it was Gyp's turn to wait, and in the waiting he looked briefly at Little Boy; and Little Boy looked back, warmly, and Gyp was relieved that Little Boy was not pained by this talk. He was, as always, in the hands of others, and this thing he had done was in the hands of others, and implicitly he expected no harm in these particular hands.

Big Meadow said slowly: "It happens pretty funny. That Moses Crease he's bangin' on the door, you know, an' we all knowin' it's him, you know, and we scairt. We scairt to open that door, you know, but that Little Boy, he can't understand so he's openin' that door, you know, before we can stop him. An' that Moses Crease he's got that knife, you know, an' he's grabbin' at Little Boy. That Little Boy he's scairt so bad but he's can't get away, you know, so he's don't even know how he's doin' it he's just grabbin' at that knife and they fallin' off them steps. I don't think Little Boy can figure what he's doin', you know, it's just happen while he's so scairt, he's doin' it all without he's thinkin'. He's so strong that Little Boy, you know, an' he's got that knife from Moses he don't even get cut, an' when he's gettin' up that knife is in Moses, you know. That's all how it happen. Pretty funny how it happen."

And Gyp's silence now was the silence of being stunned, not by how it had happened, for how in God's world could it have happened any other way, but by all that he had let happen afterward through not knowing, through accepting the impossible assumption that had come to him about deliberation and intent.

And then a surge of anger swept through him. He did not

know the origins of the anger, but he felt it, indiscriminately, against them all, himself as well. He got up from the fire and walked away, not knowing what else to do. His hands shook, and in a little while, some yards away from the others, he let himself down to the ground again.

He was not sure how much time had passed or when she had followed, but he became aware that Annie was beside him.

"Why the hell didn't he tell me?"

"You wouldn't let him."

"He told me Little Boy killed him. He could have told me then *how* he killed him. He just said with a knife, and I thought . . ." and Gyp stopped, realizing now how impossible it was even to give words to what he had thought.

He started again: "Do you know what that means? That means that Little Boy couldn't possibly get time, for God's sake. It was a plain bloody accident in self-defense and panic. Even *I* know that much. Didn't *you* realize that?"

Annie looked at him for a long while, and even in the half light he felt the penetration of the looking, and he sensed the transgression of his demand. Then she said: "How can that old man know about that? How can we know about that? He was tryin' to tell you, and you wouldn't let him. You stopped him. When you wouldn't let him tell you he thought it was like the law is so bad you can't kill somebody even he's goin' to kill you."

"*You* could have told me."

"The old man said you told him not to tell you. If he can't tell you, I can't tell you, and we so scared, we don't know what to do. The police come so quick and we got to hide Little Boy. At least we got to hide him till we can find out how bad it's goin' to be. When you wouldn't help us, we don't know what to do."

Gyp wanted to accept that, but there was one small anomaly in the way, and since everybody now was dealing in whole truths he decided to put it up for inspection.

"Why," he asked, "if the old man was so damned scared, did it all strike him so bloody funny? I mean, sticking Little Boy in *my* cellar and laughing at me when I'm trying to get Shaw out of the way and I'm just *begging* him to have enough sense to put Little Boy someplace else."

A smile crept onto Annie's face, and because she had come very close to him he could see the sparkle of the laughter dancing below the surface of her eyes.

Then she looked down and toyed bashfully with the cuff of her short sleeve, stifling, as she did so, a giggle, just a small one that bubbled from her throat.

Then: "The old man has a hard life. It's like that for us, we have a hard life. Lot of trouble, all the time. So the old man has to make joke too, 'specially when trouble is really bad. Our people is like that. You watch men diggin' grave. They makin' joke all the time. It's how they stand it, all their trouble."

That all added up for Gyp. He'd never seen nor even imagined a place that suffered so much untimely death and grief as the village.

And he knew of himself that when everything went against him—when the hay was bad and the winter was long and the cows were poor and the whole substance of his two-dollar ranch was on the verge of starvation, and he'd stay up all night to nurse a sick cow that for all his effort would forthwith die on him in the morning—when it was like that, it all seemed somehow outrageously funny, and the cow dying was the punch line in a long and continuous joke.

Which didn't mean that he didn't care about the cow and the misery for her of dying; and when he sometimes let himself just a little bit ask the why of a thing like that, he would guess that if it didn't strike you funny, it would probably kill you, too—though it might take a little time, having to be repeated through the too many winters of your life.

Big Meadow Charlie obviously was wiser in these matters than Gyp. He didn't just let the joke happen, this joke of existence that makes it possible for you to live when so much is dead set against you; he actually helped it along, by God.

There was just one more thing. "What did you have in mind yesterday morning when you ended up turning Little Boy out of my root cellar? That is to start with, before you got that idea?"

"We were goin' to get Petersen away from there some way and move Little Boy."

"That was a nice idea."

"But I got scared when you said you were goin' to pull out. I know Little Boy has to give up sometime anyway, so it was all I could think of to stop you."

"You weren't only scared. You were like a hornet's nest after you hit it with the mower."

Gyp had by now stretched himself out on the pine grass on his side with a forearm propping his head, and this time when Annie began to laugh she didn't suppress it. She let it go completely and then, as though weak with it, she fell forward from where she knelt beside Gyp and turned him onto his back as she landed on him. Then she continued with the laughing, lying almost fully on top of him; and she only stemmed the laughing when, in a little while, she kissed him.

Then Gyp interrupted her, for there was more yet that wanted saying. She lay beside him to listen as he explained: "I don't think there is now any problem for Little Boy. I'll go back in the morning and explain to Petersen how it happened, and even from me I think he might believe it. And he'll believe it anyway when he hears it from Big Meadow and meets Little Boy.

"But that's not the problem any longer. The problem now is

that Petersen has an ironclad case against me for persistent and devious obstruction of the police. At least I guess he has. I'm no expert on the law, but my hunch is all in that direction, and I sure don't intend to ask that lean bastard to find out."

"But he won't mind now it's not bad for Little Boy."

"I kind of think he will mind *even more* now that it's not bad for Little Boy. That will mean that there's even less excuse for it. But apart from that, Petersen doesn't like me. Men like Petersen do not, generally, like men like me. He thinks I'm some kind of a low-grade bastard because I live with an Indian woman, even part time."

"You are."

"I'm what?"

"A low-grade bastard because you live with an Indian woman part time."

Guilt sliced Gyp, hotly, and for a long while he said nothing, hoping the subject would go away. It was the first time Annie had ever given words to the injustice he perpetrated, the injustice to which he himself never gave words, even in the secrecy of his feelings, where mostly he hid things rather than acknowledge them.

Annie helped him by going back to where they had been before she had jolted him. "Why do white people think there's somethin' wrong with makin' love?"

"They don't, exactly. At least they don't think they do. What they say is that you got to be married first."

"It's the same thing. You got to think there's somethin' wrong with it to start with or you wouldn't have to think you got to get a piece of paper from the government and a bunch of talk in front of the priest to make it right."

"I think maybe you got a point. But I don't generally think about problems as complicated as whether something I want to do that doesn't bother anybody else can possibly be wrong.

I only know that guys like Petersen, who have nice, steady jobs and live nice, steady lives and get what they need from a nice, steady, legally hitched-up wife, have a way of looking down on guys like me, and I guess what bothers me is that when they do it, godammit, I actually *feel* like I'm an inferior bastard, and that makes me sore."

"White people been doin' that to Indians for a long time. And they doin' it for so long, Indians start believin' it, just like you."

"Yeh. I see what you mean. I never thought of that before. That's a bitch, isn't it?"

She didn't answer, but she pulled herself tightly against him and kissed the side of his face with her open mouth. Feeling the hotness and the moisture together on his skin, he wondered how she knew, so instinctively, how to do just exactly that.

And she said: "With a white guy like Petersen does it make you lower 'cause it's an Indian woman?"

Gyp didn't have to think about that, but he pretended for a while that he did. Then he said, simply: "Yeh, I guess so."

And when in the stillness of their holding together she spoke again, it was in a voice so small it seemed to shrink from its own sound, and he could barely hear her words. She said: "Sometimes they call it squaw man."

Which left them both very alone in the silence of their hurt, and the hurt was not from anything they'd said but from the judgments that had caught up to them, which were imbedded already in what the world had conveyed to Annie about herself, and which Gyp did not know how to deny because he'd never had to deal with them himself.

For a long while they said nothing more. When they spoke again it was because the advancing night had made them cold, and they needed to fetch their bedrolls. Gyp brought his from where he'd put the saddles, and she fetched hers from the leanto, and they put their bedding together, using Gyp's chaps and a scrap of canvas for a ground sheet. They held each other quietly through the night, restrained from undressing and making love perhaps by the nearness of the others in the camp, but more likely by the intrusion into their privacy of what still others, though more remote and with less right, would think.

It was in the morning after they had eaten and had drunk extra cups of coffee by the warmth of the open fire and Gyp had his horse—not the good one Little Boy had taken, but the scrubby one he'd been reduced to—saddled and ready, that Gyp did the one more thing he had to do before he could rest again inside.

He sat on his heels beside Big Meadow and, squinting against the smoke that drifted from the fire into their faces, said the awkward words: "Big Meadow, I am sorry. I didn't know I made it so hard for you. If I knew, I wouldn't make it so hard for you. I am kind of a dumb bastard, and sometimes I cannot help what I do."

And the old man looked at him with an infinite gentleness, born perhaps more than anything else from his own long experience of very often not being able to help the things he did, and out of the gentleness a smile broke and then a little laugh and then a huge laugh; and when Annie looked up in surprise from the other side of the fire from where she washed dishes, the pair of them were laughing with the tears running down their faces as though the endless joke of their luckless existence had unexpectedly discovered one of the finest of its moments, a punch line of excellence, built on the uncharitable grist of unhappy truth.

Gyp had difficulty mounting up and making his parting instruction, but he did manage it.

"Big Meadow," he said, "I have to talk some more to

Petersen, and I'll be back. Whatever the hell you do, don't go anywhere."

And they laughed some more, for that, too, was funny beyond all reason.

XVIII

Petersen had done commendably well in the camp by the time Gyp arrived back there. He'd made and eaten breakfast and washed up after it and put the camp and gear into the sort of order that Gyp would have, preparatory to packing up and setting off.

But for himself, he did not appear to have done quite so well. Perhaps it was coming on him freshly after the night away that helped Gyp realize for the first time what a difference it made to Petersen to be removed from the means of his impeccability. His uniform was rumpled and soiled from the trail and the camp. His face carried the stubble now of going on three days, and though he'd brought the means of shaving without electric power—brush, soap, and safety razor —Gyp supposed he was dissuaded from using it by the absence of a basin to work out of. Even his short cropped hair had managed to elude a little the rigid discipline usually imposed on it, and Petersen's attempt to hide it under the forage cap was not totally successful.

For a brief moment Gyp sensed the man behind the uniform and was surprised by the feeling of it—rather as a child is by the discovery that a strict teacher, encountered hitherto only in the classroom, actually does things like ordinary people, such as eating and sleeping and going to the store. Petersen had been so totally policeman that it was mildly surprising to see that if he didn't shave he'd grow stubble, just like Gyp.

Gyp brought a few sticks in to replenish the fire and put fresh water in the billy to heat for tea.

Then he joined Petersen by the fire and made his opener. "I have been to Big Meadow's camp."

"I presumed as much. How is Little Boy?"

"Well, that's what I was going to talk to you about. But don't be in such a hurry all the time. I can't operate at your speed."

"I don't think you can operate at any speed. But do your best in your own good time."

Gyp kept a deliberate silence for a while, not to think in, because thinking wasn't likely to help much at that moment, but because it was about the only way left to assert some power of choice. If Petersen wouldn't wait for Gyp to say what he was going to talk about, by God at least he was going to wait for Gyp to decide when.

After this futile surge of willfulness had about run itself out, Gyp started again. "Let's suppose . . ."

"Let's not suppose a damn thing," Petersen cut him off. "I had my fill of that a couple of days ago. Just tell me about Little Boy."

"What," Gyp said slowly, "would you like to know?"

"Where he is and how I can take him into custody without doing him any harm. And without having to play this tiresome game of yours, either."

"You don't improve with age, Petersen. But I'm an easy bastard to get along with. Tell you what I'll do. I'll lend you that horse you've been riding, and I'll lend you the pack mare and the camp outfit. You go find Little Boy yourself, and *you* figure out how you can take him into custody without doing him any harm. I will not interfere with you at all. I will just go home and forget this whole damned business."

"You overlook, Sandhouse, that you have some things of your own to explain to a judge, quite apart from whatever Little Boy has to account for, presuming he can account for anything. Like the fact that if you hadn't hidden him, he would have been in lawful custody several days ago. Without all this stupid nonsense in the bargain."

"I told you I didn't have anything to do with that. Him being hidden in my cellar."

"And I told you I didn't believe you. But let's quit wrangling, and if I'm partly to blame for that, please realize that I'm not used to having to play cowboys and Indians across half the Chilcotin bush to do a very ordinary piece of police work that should have been wound up in about two hours the first day I came to the village."

Gyp thought about that, and the human quality in Petersen emerged again by virtue of the thinking. So Gyp then said: "I'll make it short. We can pick up Little Boy any time we like. In fact, I'll bring him here, or we can meet him at the village. But first I have to tell you something I only learned myself last night."

"Yes?" Petersen, in that one intent word, displayed his immediate realization, uncanny to Gyp, that what Gyp had learned had thrown a whole new meaning on everything. He leaned forward as though to capture the information, as if it might try to escape as Gyp would tell it.

Gyp hated it, but in that moment he was awed by him. And he said: "It was accidental, Little Boy killing Moses. Moses had a knife and grabbed at Little Boy. Somehow Little Boy got the knife away, and when they fell off the porch together the knife went into Moses." And then: "It had to be like that. Little Boy couldn't do it except by accident."

Petersen's eyes stayed on Gyp's face for a long while, and then he said: "I believe you. For once you're telling the truth.

But why didn't they explain that to me at the first and save all this chasing around?"

The answer to that, Gyp realized, was too complicated for him to begin to explain, tied up as it was in his own refusal to listen to Big Meadow Charlie the morning after it had all taken place.

So he just said: "They were afraid."

"I see."

The two men fell into silence then, each of them in a private silence, and Gyp's silence was largely blank. When Petersen spoke again to ask what Gyp suggested they do next, Gyp had to think it out as he offered it.

"Well, I guess you'd better stay here and I'll go fetch Little Boy. Also, I'm worried about Shaw. It's three days since I left him, and I think he could get himself into enough trouble in one day to last me a week fixing it up afterward. So I think I also have to go fetch him."

"Forget it. Not until Little Boy and I and whoever is traveling with Little Boy are all back at Big Meadow and I can get the statements I need to dispose of this business."

"It's that simple?"

"It's that simple. It's that simple for Little Boy. It's not that simple for you though, Sandhouse. Need I explain more? You lied, you obstructed, you misled, you . . ."

"Enough! Godammit. Don't lay it on with a fork."

Then Petersen said, largely to himself: "And it's not going to be that simple for Shaw, either, damn him and his cockeyed imagination. He can't go out on a ham-handed B&E into a hardware store without pretending he's onto an international conspiracy to take over the tool trade."

Gyp had a moment of sympathy for Shaw. Petersen was, after all, a hard man, and hard men do not have much patience with fools. Still, it was not his business, and he did not dwell on it for long.

He said: "Stay here. I'll fetch Little Boy and we'll go back to Big Meadow together."

Then he mounted up and left. He had known before he left that his responsibility for Shaw and his fear that in three days it was almost a certainty that Shaw would in some way manage to get into grief would compel him to take the little time he would need just to call by the old cabin where he had left Shaw, before going on to bring Little Boy and Big Meadow Charlie and Annie back to his own camp. From there he would lead them all to Big Meadow.

But he had felt it hopeless to try to explain that to Petersen so that the intention could be legitimate. And anyway, what was a little more deceit now?

So within five minutes down the trail he had cut northward to pick up the track that would take him out to the cabin. In less than an hour he was there.

But Shaw wasn't, not any longer. Neither Shaw, nor the saddle horse, not a damned thing to say when or why he'd left.

XIX

Gyp did a fast reconnaissance, but it was not useful. He could find no clear tracks on top of the assortment of others, his own included, that had been along these several converging trails recently. So he was forced to conclude that Shaw— or his horse—had had compelling reasons to strike off the trails, for a short distance at any rate, and pine grass and moss do not retain imprints fit for the use of limited trackers like Gyp.

Gyp headed for Big Meadow at a mile-eating trot, and he

was there in little over half an hour. Shaw was not there, neither at the village nor at Upper Meadow.

Gyp rode back, still at that persistent and urgent pace, to the camp where he'd left Petersen, and he dismounted right by the fire where Petersen still waited, though with the gathering heat of the day he'd let the blaze go nearly out.

Gyp spoke at once, before Petersen had any chance. "Shaw is gone. He's left the cabin where I stashed him."

"Maybe he got tired of waiting and went to Big Meadow."

"No. I checked that out right away. He's not there. He's lost."

Petersen's face froze with a startling suddenness into visible fury. He glared at Gyp, who waited for the explosion of angry words, though he was far from sure what was truly the source of Petersen's rage.

But the words came coldly: "When will you quit lying to me?"

"I'm not, dammit. He's gone."

"I *know* that." Then exasperation joined the anger. "Let me spell it out for you. You told me you were going to get Little Boy. But instead you intended to get Shaw, *even* after I said to leave him until we'd got Little Boy. And your other lies are getting bigger. You said you left Shaw because he couldn't ride in. But you have been no more than three hours going to wherever you left Shaw, then to the village and then back here. If Shaw had been raw to the flesh you could have made him endure that much. You deliberately ditched him to get him out of the way. Need I ask why? In all your innocence? And after all the trouble you have put me to, you're still lying to me, as late as this morning when even in your addled brain there can't be any good reason for it."

The exasperation had the better part of the anger now, and Gyp wondered how much more Petersen could take. Even collected men like Petersen, given to imposing their will on the most chilling of crises, must have a breaking point.

Gyp said to him, quietly, "It's serious about Shaw. We could lose him. Really lose him. I mean . . ." and the words trailed off because the ultimate possibility did not bear being spoken.

Petersen stared at him, as if in concentration to find a sane course through his own anger. Then he asked: "What do you want to do?"

"Look for Shaw. I'll go back to Big Meadow's camp and take him with me. I'll take the pack mare and this camp outfit. You take your saddle horse and give him his head. He'll bring you into Upper Meadow, and you can wait for me there. When I get Shaw we'll all come back and you'll have Little Boy. I promise."

"All right."

And within minutes Gyp had the camp struck and the mare packed and Petersen's horse saddled with Petersen's bedroll lashed behind, and had given Petersen the simple directions that would set his horse on a homeward course to Upper Meadow.

Then just on parting Gyp put a question that was still important, though peripheral now to the loss of Shaw. Still, he wanted confirmation on the point. "Supposing it is like I explained it to you, and it is, you know, will there have to be any charge at all against Little Boy?"

"No. And on that one thing, I do believe you."

"Thanks."

Then Petersen raised a peripheral concern of his own. But he said it with feeling, almost imploringly, and Gyp was taken rather by surprise. He asked: "Is there a bathtub around your place by any chance?"

"No. Sorry about that. In hot weather I wash in the creek. In cold weather I don't wash much at all, but when I do, I heat water in a bucket and spill it over me. We tend to live a little high in these parts."

"Oh. Well, just thought I'd ask. Damn, but I'd like to be clean again."

Which was how they left it.

XX

Big Meadow said just two words when Gyp told him at his camp about Shaw's disappearance and about Gyp's own substantial anxiety about him. There had been little in all this disorder that was directly of Gyp's making—it was all largely of his bungling maybe, but not of his making—but this one misfortune, this losing of the inept greenhorn of a policeman, this lay very squarely on Gyp's conscience.

Big Meadow said: "Pascal's Lake." And that was so obvious, once said, that Gyp could not understand why he had not thought of it himself; for if anything was certain in the incongruousness of Shaw being matched with that particular gelding, it was that the gelding would manage the partnership.

And if there was anything certain about that particular gelding it was his ineradicable desire to return to the swamp grass of his birthplace.

Gyp knew that you could be riding him at the end of a long day, and not an hour out of Upper Meadow and a manger full of hay, and if you should dismount to deal with the constant shaking down of your bladder by his rattling gait, he would, in that moment of your remounting with one foot in the stirrup and the other swinging over his back—just then, when you were unable to attend to the reins to direct his head—he would turn right about and make yardage for Pascal's Lake to beat hell before you'd get him under control again. He would do it as though all the journeys you had hitherto made with him were merely preludes to that final very personal task just then accomplished and, that done, surely at last it was time to go home, and not to Upper Meadow, but home to Pascal's Lake.

The possibility that Shaw would be able to direct him elsewhere, supposing Shaw knew where else to direct him, was not even worth consideration.

So Big Meadow's camp was struck, and its limited ingredients were tied behind saddles, and they all set off. But it was a long day's ride from Big Meadow to Pascal's Lake at the best of times, and though they were an hour's ride in the right direction to start with, a good half of the day had been used already.

So they camped perhaps an hour short of their destination, and making use now of Gyp's outfit, they camped comfortably. And then in that comfort, in the time after eating and cleaning up that belonged to talk and to looking in long stretches into the flames of the campfire, Gyp touched just briefly on those other matters that had been forgotten in the hunt for Shaw.

"I have explained to Petersen how it happened. He says there'll be no charge against Little Boy. He'll just have to have statements from everybody who was there when it happened."

Annie's anxieties had moved already in quite another direction. She hardly acknowledged Gyp's announcement.

She asked: "What about you?"

Gyp considered that, but the considering didn't tell him much. Still, he passed on what little it did. "I don't know about me. Not much, except that I have given Petersen a very bad time, if you look at it from where he sits, and he doesn't have any reason I can think of to like me. So if he can stick me with anything, I am kind of expecting to be stuck. But maybe not. It's maybe turned into such a bad dream kind of thing for him, all he'll want to do is forget it instead of hauling me into court, where he'll have to go through it all again, telling it to the judge. I would suggest that to him, except I don't think he would believe that I'm thinking only about what's best for him. Maybe I should figure out some way to mess it up for him even worse than it is already. I ought to be able to turn out a real nightmare with a little scheming. Look how well I've done so far without even trying."

Gyp's idle fantasy had about run out of entertainment value for him, so he discarded it and settled onto his back in the firelight and gazed up through the spaces between the tree-tops at the stars. Then in afterthought: "I almost feel sorry for that hard-nosed bastard. Funny how it almost makes him the same as the rest of us, being stuck out here where he can't get a bath and a shave. Sort of takes away his power. Was the last thing he said to me, did I have a bathtub around my place. Almost like he'd forgotten everything else."

Which was all that was said that Gyp could recall later to account for the brazen shenanigan that Annie's imagination led her then to undertake, and that she must have worked out in all its magnificent detail by the time she did her own disappearing act the very next day.

XXI

They had broken camp and headed off and come by the edge of the meadow at Pascal's Lake, where they had reined up so Gyp might share his relief at the sight of smoke from the pipe of the old abandoned cabin and of the gelding grazing blissfully in the meadow, when she left.

Having stayed with them just so long as needed to fix the fact that Shaw was indeed to be found here, she turned in the trail without a word and set off back in the direction of Big Meadow, pressing her horse to a fast, persistent trot.

Gyp queried Big Meadow: "Now what do you make of that?"

But Big Meadow said nothing, that being the most economical way of dealing with the fact that he did not make anything of it at all, and so they left it, unmade of, as it were, these two men whose need to account for anything even slightly less than obvious was sharply limited.

They started up their horses and, followed by Little Boy and the pack mare, set off to cover the two hundred yards across the meadow that separated them from the cabin. Arriving there they dismounted and, by unspoken agreement, Gyp went first to the door.

"Shaw!" he shouted. "You there?"

On the answering shout from within, Gyp opened the door and stood in the doorway while he took in the scene within.

The cabin was dim in the way of many an old homestead cabin, only one small window (limited by the inconvenience of having been brought in by pack horse) letting in just a little of the daylight. This particular window, being on the side away from the approaching trail, did not even offer the possibility of seeing someone coming.

"You all right?"

"Sure. I'm all right. Found this old cabin here and just doing fine. Good thing you got here though. How are you making out? See any sign of Little Boy?"

It was almost beyond believing, even for Gyp, who was prone to accept anything his eyes conveyed to him.

For Shaw *was* all right. Not only was he all right, he was thriving. He had shaved, and his uniform, fully on, looked unaccountably neat, and the cabin obviously had been put in some order. The wonder of it all so arrested Gyp's attention that he overlooked that Shaw had asked him questions. Instead, he asked a few of his own.

"You alone?"

"Absolutely."

"Been here long?"

"Couple of days. Figured you must have got tied up at something, so I decided I'd better get on with it. Just a matter of following these old trails around and checking out the old cabins."

"You aren't worried you might get lost?"

"Oh, no. All you have to do is let your horse have his head and he'll take you home. Old trick the sergeant in training camp told me about. Never forgotten it."

"I see. You got any grub left?"

"A little. That was going to be my problem if you didn't catch up to me pretty soon."

It was magnificent, this imposition of Shaw's imagination on his reality with its consequent reordering. Nothing less could account for Shaw not being in the blind panic that his own ignorance would have inspired in any ordinary mind.

Gyp decided to see if there was not perhaps a reality of such proportions that Shaw's imagination could not refashion it into a stock role within the grand drama of his career in the Force.

So he said: "I got Little Boy."

Shaw froze and he was, in that moment, absolutely real. He asked, hoarsely: "Where?"

Gyp turned back in the doorway to motion to Little Boy, and then stepped in the cabin to let Little Boy use the passage. Little Boy did and he filled it, completely, as he stooped to come through it.

Shaw turned white. His words barely made it across the cabin. "That's Little Boy?"

"That's Little Boy."

"Tell him . . . tell him he's under arrest."

"Little Boy. You're under arrest."

Little Boy smiled in the happy, congenial way that he had in the potato bin and at the campfire when Gyp had asked of Big Meadow the question that by all reckoning should have been horrible beyond all bearing but wasn't. When told to hide, Little Boy would hide; when told to run, he would take flight; when told to stand under arrest he would do that, too, and all with the same implicit trust born of the kind of innocence of which only such as Little Boy are capable.

Shaw swallowed, with difficulty. He had not reckoned on the sheer size of Little Boy, and the obvious meekness of the prisoner helped only a very little.

Gyp decided he had better help Shaw a little farther or Shaw might remain frozen forever where he stood.

So he explained: "Been a few things happened. Turns out Little Boy isn't guilty of anything much. Killed the guy in self-defense. Petersen knows the story and he says no sweat, but says Little Boy's got to be taken in to make a statement. He's waiting for us at my place. And Little Boy, he's harmless."

"Oh."

"But you got to take him in."

"Yes. Well, we'll do that. We'll take him in right away. No question of that. Where'd you find him?"

"He was camped down the trail a piece. Him and Big Meadow."

"Well, better get your outfit ready. We got to move."

"My outfit is sort of already ready. Incidentally, I'm in a little trouble too."

"How is that?" Shaw's eyes narrowed and he prepared himself to receive the admission of wrongdoing from this unexpected source. You can never tell.

"I was hiding him out."

"You were hiding him out?"

"Yeh. All the time you were at my place. When we went into the bush to look for him I was throwing you off the trail."

Shaw weighed that. Then he spoke in the clipped phrases of command: "Sandhouse."

"Yes."

"You're under arrest."

"Yes." Then in afterthought: "Yes, sir."

"Sandhouse."

"Yes, sir."

"Big Meadow. Is he involved too?"

"Not really. Not so it's serious. Anyway, you need a scout, and that old Indian, he knows this country like he was raised in it. Fact, he was."

"Good. All right, Sandhouse. I don't want any trouble from either of you. And we'll pull out right away."

"Yes, sir."

"And Sandhouse. And you, too, Little Boy."

Gyp said his usual yes, sir, and Little Boy smiled in that eager way that marked the inclusion in the company of those he could trust of this new wise man, and Shaw said to them both: "No hard feelings, you know. My duty, and I must carry it out."

"We understand."

"Good. Have you got some grub? I'm hungry."

"Right away."

Then they forgot all about who was arrested and what the hell for and settled down to an enormous heap of grub out of Gyp's pack boxes.

And Shaw shared dried deer meat and billy can tea with his new friends with such genuine pleasure in them all that Gyp was led to wonder how so real a person could live such an unreal even if gloriously adventurous life up there in the zeniths of his mind.

His eager sincerity was not lost either on Big Meadow, who remarked to Gyp when there happened a moment alone with him to do it in, that it was one damned good thing that Gyp had put Shaw on that Pascal's Lake gelding, because you sure wouldn't want to lose a nice guy like that.

And then they fetched and saddled that gelding and rolled up Shaw's bit of outfit and made their way out of there, but all in all they'd wasted enough time that they had to camp a couple of hours short of Upper Meadow.

Which was just as well, for Annie had counted on it.

If they'd come in that evening they'd have interrupted the something rather exceptional that she had arranged for Petersen.

XXII

It was a long ride back to Upper Meadow in what Annie had left of the day after leaving Gyp and her father and Little Boy at the edge of the meadow at Pascal's Lake. But even though she pressed her horse, in the constant pace of the trail there was still time to think; and Annie found herself absorbed again in the puzzle of her own self and the contradictory world she lived in.

It had often occurred to Annie, since she had come to know her own self so well, that such a lot went on inside her for the little she was ever able to let out for the understanding of others.

But what could you do?

You have these precious old people of your very own with whom you have the most perfect understandings of love without any need to let on the complications that life has put inside you.

Then you have the rest of the village, these few people in this only place in the world where you can really know who you are. But so much has happened to you in your growing years away that there is more not known about you than is, even in this only place in the world that knows you.

Then you have all those white people you have met. But even with those few who really cared, there was always that risk, too big to be taken, that in the final disclosing of your self you would come up against, at the very least, the inability, the unaware inability, to know you, perhaps even the cold refusal.

And finally you have this impossible man you have fallen in love with, and you would gladly tell him every secret in your heart, but he is so afraid of what lies inside his own that you cannot talk with him of anything that matters.

Annie could be easily hurt. She was hurt now by the way that white judgment had reached even into this refuge where they lived and made its put-down on Gyp and on herself and on the very condition of being an Indian, using, as its excuse, as it always would, the fact that they were lovers.

It was not that she felt threatened by the judgment, for she had already reached a kind of certainty in herself that defied any claim to validity of what was implied in that judgment; it was just that it hurt.

But she was sound, and if that meant that the rest of the world, especially the white world, was haywire, then the rest of the world, especially the white world, *was* haywire, and that was the way of it.

Her certainty of her own soundness was as clear and precious as the memory of the first nine years of her life—and the two, she knew in that way that she knew herself, were inextricably bound together.

114

The very earliest memory she could recall was typical of those years. They were all in the tent, her father and her mother and the veritable jumble of brothers and sisters and cousins—anybody could be cousins—and herself, though she supposed now that the remembering of the other children in that first incident must have been added on later.

But she was in bed on top of the huge mountain of chest and stomach that her father consisted of mostly, and she was naked against his skin and enveloped in the warmth of him, and for some reason he laughed, and in the laughing rolled her off, and she slid down between him and her mother. And the memory was of the delicious comfort of the two immense bodies enclosing her, and of the warmth, the powerful, enveloping warmth.

All those summers of her early life had been spent in camps. As soon in the season as there was any excuse for it and green grass enough to feed the horses, Big Meadow would load his wagon with a jumble of tent and gear and grub and the means of securing more grub—rifle, ammunition, and fish net. Then he'd hitch the team to the wagon, and some of the family would pile on board, while others—the children of ten and twelve and thereabouts—would follow behind on the three or four saddle horses of Big Meadow's occasional possession, and they would set off.

The ostensible reasons for the trekking varied with the seasons—netting fish in the stream mouth at Mowloo Lake, putting up the little hay that grew at Three Mile Meadow, killing fat buck deer on the fir ridges far to the west of Big Meadow and drying the meat in strips on racks in the sun, picking blueberries by the bucketful and mostly eating them there in the camp in delicious sour sweet mouthfuls, hunting moose up at the headwaters of Whistler Creek in the early fall and rendering down the huge slabs of back fat into large tin containers for the coming winter.

And all these were important reasons, too, for they had much to do with how Big Meadow made his living. But sometimes he trekked even when there was no other purpose for it than just the traveling and the camping and the enormous indifference it all made possible to whatever else the world might expect of him.

Annie cherished her memories of it all. The days were never counted through those long summers, and only the schooling of the fish, the readiness of the hay to cut, the fattening of the bucks, the ripening of the blueberries, and the advancing frosts of the fall were heeded.

They camped in beautiful places, for the vast plateau country in which they roamed was a grand mixture of both open and wooded country, flat prairie and rolling hills, small lakes and sparkling streams, and a wagon could not run out of places to go.

They camped by the lakes and the streams, sometimes in the open to avoid the mosquitoes, sometimes in the forest for protection from the advancing weather, and always where they could hobble and picket the horses in abundant feed.

They were many in the family—Annie could not say then or now how many—and sometimes they used more than one tent, especially when they were occasionally joined by one of the older girls and her husband.

And with so many, there was an inevitable closeness in their living. But, as Annie realized on looking back, because they did not have the obsession about privacy and hiding from the view of others that white people not only suffer from but have infected Indians with, the closeness was entirely comfortable.

Annie remembered how beautiful their bodies were.

Her father had always been huge, and the hugeness of him was like his gentleness with a child. He would lie uncovered on his blankets when the stove was set inside in wet weather, making the interior of the tent fearfully hot, and a baby would crawl about him and climb on him and he would hold the little one with his huge weathered hands on top of his great middle, and it was as though the infant sat on an enormous mound of love.

Annie's mother was large, too, but it was a different kind of largeness, a soft largeness, a body of many folds of comfort that you loved to lie next to, and no matter how many of you there were, there seemed always to be as much of lying next to her as you needed.

Annie liked to watch her mother bathe in the shallow water by the lakeshore in the hot sun, when the wetness would make her skin glisten in its many folds.

And there was the different beauty of her older sisters who, like herself, were very slim and seemed ever so long-legged— and they were especially beautiful in their firm, curved behinds and the high roundness, slightly pointed, of their breasts. As she grew toward the end of those idyllic years Annie sensed how the profound excitement of the very creation of life was in all their bodies, but especially in the slim, firm bodies of her older sisters.

And in the impudence, too, of her brother two years younger, the one between herself and Little Boy, who liked to race up and down the pebbled beach at the fish camp with nothing on, splashing in and out of the water as he ran, stopping to heave cupped handfuls of it onto anyone who might be lying in the sun. His lithe, brown body shone in the summer sun, and he delighted in himself. He would sometimes make himself erect with a gleeful sense of mischief, and once Annie saw her father and mother notice it and laugh quietly between themselves over something her mother said about it.

In the last of those first nine years of Annie's life Little Boy had been the baby in the camp—he was born when

Annie was seven—and his peculiar dependence had been fairly evident from the very beginning. He had been a large baby and had grown rapidly, but his mind never kept pace with his body, and so from the start he had endeared himself to them all by his extra need and by the obliging way he responded to their care with his affection.

In good years they used to spend the best part of six months coming or going or camped in some happy place, and then the rest of the year snug and crowded in the cabin at Big Meadow Reserve, living on the fall-killed meat and then the dried foods put up in the summer.

It had all come to an end in the year that Annie was nine. She hadn't realized it then, but both the priest and the Indian agent had been putting constant pressure on Big Meadow to put his children in school. Now, growing a little old perhaps for the considerable work involved in his seasonal nomadism, he finally acceded.

That fall his five children between seven and fourteen years of age went out to the Indian residential school near Williams Lake.

It had been as hard for him as if he had been persuaded that he should not let his babies, one by one as they found the strength in their little legs, stomp all over his belly in the tent in the mornings. But the pervasiveness of the white man was such that even in the refuge of his summer wandering, Big Meadow could not escape the belief that the only life that would be left for anyone to live in a few brief years would be on the white man's terms. And the school near Williams Lake would teach his children white men's skills.

He believed he was doing what was right for his children, and that it was only his own weakness that had prevented him doing it earlier—his weakness that he had not been able to give them up.

Annie, of course, did not come to know all this until many

years later when her father, more than to any of the others, told her, in little pieces here and there and never quite directly, how torn he had been by their going.

She only knew at the time how frightening it was to see the tears come to his eyes when he gave them over to the bus that had come down the almost impassable road that rarely saw a motor vehicle, to fetch them.

XXIII

Only Big Meadow had held out so late against sending his children away for the long school year—even at Christmas, unless the parents fetched them (and no one had the means), the children could not come home—and so Annie had heard the others speak of the school and tell things of their time there.

But she had had no idea what it meant, and she had not even tried to imagine it, for it had seemed such a distant and alien place that though it might happen to others to be sent there, it could never happen to her.

She was sick from the journey and numbed by the terrifying realization that no matter how much she hurt, she could not go to her father or her mother, because they were not there.

She had been taken away from them.

She stood with her brothers and sisters in a cluster beside the bus and stared at the frightening buildings, which were big beyond belief.

The other children knew where to go and they all left, and then the bus drove away. They had been getting on the bus the last time that Annie had still been able to look at her father, and if she had run back she could have touched him again.

That had been yesterday, and they had traveled all night and Annie did not know how much of today had gone by. She only knew distance in how far you could come in a day with horses, and so she did not know how far away her father was now, or even in what direction.

She turned away from the buildings, and there were open fields that she could look across. They were very different from the big open of the meadow where the men cut the hay in the summer, but she tried her best to make them all look the same.

At one place at the edge of the open there was a long stretch of willow bush that was the same as the edge of the lake at Big Meadow. She fixed her eyes on the long line of willows, and she wondered if the meadow where the men cut hay in the summer could be on the other side of it.

In her mind she pictured her father on his horse, and she tried to take the picture from her mind and put it by the willows. It would only take a few minutes for him to get to where they stood.

Maybe when he saw them standing there he would hurry. She would touch him as soon as he got down from his horse and hold onto the fringes of his old buckskin coat. She wished she had held onto the fringes of his coat when the bus had come. If she had held tightly, she might not have had to go.

She was still trying to take the picture of her father from her mind and put it by the distant stretch of willows. If she could make him real she could touch him.

She began to cry. She could not stop from crying any longer, and the willows where she wanted her father to appear on his horse blurred through the tears.

A nun came to get them. She spoke to them in English, and though they didn't understand the words, they knew they were meant to follow. The nun held out her hand for Annie to take, but Annie did not take it. It was a thin, pale hand, and it did not have any comfort in it.

Her father's hand was large and strong and brown and wrinkled from the sun, and you could hold it next to your face and it smelled of horses and leather and the smoke from the campfire.

There was not anything real now. The world had been torn away, and a dream had taken its place. But the dream was stronger than the world, and it would not let you have your people in it. It was full of white people, and even the Indians were strangers.

There was no place in the dream for Annie, but it forced her to stay there anyway.

There was nowhere in the dream for Annie to go for comfort.

Annie moved mechanically through the strangeness, and she did not know afterward how it had come about that she had been separated from the others and led to a big room.

The room was so long you could hardly see from one end to the other, and it was filled with beds.

There were many other children. There were too many other children. There was no way to know them because there were so many.

It made the aloneness worse, and Annie clutched at her face with her fingers, for she was afraid now even of her own crying.

The children saw her fingers digging into the flesh of her face, and they backed away from her. Their eyes were wide in fright. She was surrounded by their fear, and it added to her own. Her crying began to scream.

Another child screamed, and a different nun came running. She tore Annie's hands away from her face and held her powerfully in her arms, and she stayed a long time until finally Annie's crying stopped, and in the forced closeness, even against the stranger, the fear subsided.

A numbness was left, and it stayed with her.

After that, for a long time after that, Annie cried, not in the daytime, but at night in her bed, stifling the sound of it as much as she could in the blankets, because she did not want to be heard by the others and by Sister Mary, who would walk through the long rows of beds and tell the ones who were crying to keep quiet.

Annie wished that Sister Theresa could be the one to look after the girls in the dormitory, because if Sister Theresa saw someone crying, she would try to give comfort. She was the one who had stopped Annie from tearing at her face in her fear, and Annie sometimes saw tears in Sister Theresa's eyes, too, when a child was crying.

Sister Mary was straight and stiff like the long, straight rows of beds in the dormitory and the long, straight lines of tables where they ate the tasteless white food, and she smelled of soap, just like the whole school smelled of the sharp, disinfecting soap. There were no comfortable smells anywhere, and there was nothing comfortable about Sister Mary.

Annie longed for the smells of the camp and the disarray inside the tent and for the lying next to her mother; but she was learning now to force the vivid pictures of it all from her mind, because the pain of longing was more than she could bear.

For the first time in her life she had a sense of time, and the sense was of how long it would be until the hay would be almost ready to cut next early summer, which was when she would be home again; what an eternity this was when measured against her loneliness.

Annie had a little English, but it was not nearly enough to

let her understand all the things that the children were told to do. But because she was nine, everybody but the teacher in her class seemed to think she'd been at the school before and should know more English and how to act properly.

For a long time she couldn't learn how to wear the clothing all the children had to wear. Even when she watched the others and tried to do just what they did, Sister Mary would have to stop her to change something, and would scold her for it.

She got in trouble because she didn't know there was a wrong side to the stockings. She kept wearing them inside out.

She wished it was summer and she was at the fish camp.

She wouldn't have to bother with clothing at all.

She would run naked on the beach, and her body would feel good to her in the open air.

She would run into the water and then lie on her tummy on the hot pebbles. The sun would feel good on her back and her legs and her behind, and Sister Mary would not even know where she was.

XXIV

It was in looking back later that Annie realized how substantially the school was part of the life of the people of her village; to such an extent, in fact, that part of being an Indian was to go to that school, suffer its imposition on you, then, having been there and having gone back to your reserve, have the school in your memory and carry its strange legacy of the equation of pleasure with sin (and you were never quite sure how much of that you had already acquired) with you the rest of your life.

At any rate, that was how it seemed for most of the others.

But for Annie the pattern had been broken. She'd been only three years in the school when the tuberculosis in her lung had appeared in an X ray, and from the time she was twelve until she was sixteen she was in the TB hospital, and it was there that she did most of her schoolwork. Once she'd got enough English and finally figured out what the arithmetic was all about, she'd caught up her grades with no difficulty.

In fact, with little else to do in all that time in the hospital and with the help she got from the teacher because there were so few children in the hospital school, she finished grade ten and was able to go to the nurse's aide course when she was seventeen.

She'd worked for a year. But then she had finally despaired of finding any meaning in the white man's world, and she'd come back to live at Big Meadow with her parents again.

It was like walking back into her life after a long absence. The short visits over the years had let her touch it now and again, but when she had finally come back with no expectation of leaving, it was as though she had reached out and taken the hand of the child she had been when she was nine and they could now go on together, not as though all that intervening experience hadn't happened, of course, but with it all set at long last out of the way of being one's own true self.

Now she could become the woman of the child she had been.

Except that now she puzzled on the contradictions of life in a way that she believed she might never have had cause to if the child could have been left alone.

The puzzling came often and of its own accord, occupying

her mind in the hours of her otherwise uncomplicated life at
Big Meadow.

And it was with her now as she pressed her horse on the
long trail to Upper Meadow where, she was sure, she would
find Petersen.

XXV

There was, for example, all the puzzle about bodies.

She had felt so encumbered in the night clothing provided
by the school that when she grew confident enough to decide
at least that much for herself, she began to take it off after
she was in bed and the lights were out.

It felt so much better to lie naked beneath the bedding. She
could move her arms and legs freely, and her own skin felt
so good to her touch.

But Sister Mary discovered her one night when in her
sleep the blankets had fallen away from her bare shoulders,
and she was torn awake by the flashlight and the cross scold-
ing.

Sister Mary said she was sinful, but she never really understood that; she only knew she felt so much better without all
that night clothing bound around her in bed.

Another time, much later, when she'd begun to enjoy going
into the shower as a sort of distant substitute for splashing in
the shallow water of the lakeshore, she was scolded because
she had walked unclothed the long way down the dormitory
from her bed to the shower room. Sister had told her she had
no modesty at all, that she had better realize she was as
obligated as anyone else to keep herself decently covered,
and not to take her nightie off until she was ready to step in

the shower. Furthermore, she was to dry herself and put her nightie on at once when she stepped out.

It was all so oppressive, and Annie began to wonder what could possibly be so wrong with bodies.

She believed the Sisters must sleep with their heaps of clothing still on, they were so fiercely secretive about what they might look like underneath it all. You couldn't tell if they had breasts or not, the way they wore their habits. Except, that was, for the nun who worked in the dining room, for she dressed in such a way that you could see she was really, genuinely, completely flat-chested.

Annie decided that having no breasts was a very important thing for a nun, a much-wanted condition, but that only the one in the dining room hadn't any, and that all the others were stuck with having to dress their best to seem as if they hadn't any.

Annie looked forward to when she would have full, round breasts. She would try to imagine how it would feel to her hands to touch them, and what she would look like; especially she tried to picture herself standing in the shallow water of the lake at the fish camp with the sun shining on her richly colored skin. Her father and her mother would notice her, and she would be very proud of her body with her full, round breasts.

She was very glad Sister Mary could not know what she was thinking. Sister Mary would make her feel ashamed. Sister Mary was very skilled at making you feel ashamed. It was very important with Sister Mary to keep your real self a secret.

At the hospital it was very different.

Bodies came there because they were sick. You couldn't always tell by looking at them, but the tuberculosis germ had been seen in them by the X ray, and the people in the hospital worked to make the bodies well again.

Any body, it didn't matter. As long as it had the tuberculosis germ in it somewhere, they would put it in bed and give it medicine and tell it how to keep clean and what exercise to do. Then, when the body was well again, it could be sent back to wherever it had come from.

Nobody made that other kind of fuss about bodies, that fuss that implied that there was something downright shameful in bodies, and soon the bodies got used to being undressed and looked at and weighed on the scale and measured and their temperatures taken. Each body did not even mind after a while being seen by the other bodies, and sometimes even the nurses forgot the rule that the bodies were supposed to keep something on when they weren't having something done to them.

That was because the boy bodies weren't supposed to see the girl bodies—it was all right if girl bodies saw girl bodies—and one time Annie and a nurse who was always in a rush had a big laugh because in her hurry to get Annie into her bath while she went to fetch her some clean pajamas, Annie dashed a short way across the hall in what the nurse called her altogether, meaning just her skin.

It had been fun, but they didn't do it again.

But that had been exceptional, that bit of fun with the nurse, because mainly the bodies were just bodies and nobody much thought to have fun with them.

It wasn't that some of the people who worked to make the bodies well didn't care about the people who lived in the bodies; they did. But there were so many bodies, and the nurses worked on shifts; and when you badly needed someone who knew at least a little the person inside your body, she would be on another shift.

And the nurses and the other staff left their jobs sometimes and new people took their places, so that even if some of them cared about the person inside the body, the hospital itself didn't seem to.

Only Mrs. Hutchins was the one who really cared and who was always there. She had been there for longer than anyone, people used to say, and she would be there, she herself used to say, just as long as you little eggs need me.

She taught their subjects to the children of school age, and sometimes she taught older people as well who had never been to school and who wanted to learn to read and write while they were in the hospital.

She was supposed to run the little classroom for just the regular hours of school each day. But she spent far more time than that, going from room to room afterward helping each child with whatever was difficult for him or her.

And because Mrs. Hutchins cared, Annie worked hard at her schoolwork, and with all the special help she was able to catch up and really did understand the work.

When Annie's body changed and her breasts began to fill, she suddenly grew desperate about herself. Her body had been a thing to be worked on for making well for so long that it wasn't special any more. She was glad it was being made well, too, because she was very afraid of how the TB germ would damage it from inside. But now she so badly needed to go where she was special again, to the fish camp, to stand in the shallows of the lakeshore and splash the water down over her body in the sun and let the water form into little sparkling droplets on her rich brown skin, especially on her newly filling breasts.

And the only people in the world who really knew who Annie was would watch her there, and she would be a person again with a beautiful special body all her own.

She had always imagined that when her breasts began to fill she would kneel on the warm pebbles of the beach and lean forward so her breasts would fall downward from her chest and she could cup the nippled ends in the palms of her hands very lightly. Then she would close her fingertips onto her breasts and draw them gently down until they came together at the nipples.

But there was nowhere in the hospital where she could find joy in her body, and it was Mrs. Hutchins who saw her sadness and tried to help. She asked Annie if Annie could tell her what was wrong. But Annie could not make words for it, and then she was afraid that Mrs. Hutchins would be like the other white people and think that Indian people didn't have feelings, when it was only that it was impossible for them to talk about them.

But Mrs. Hutchins must have understood a lot more than Annie guessed at the time, for she didn't ask Annie to talk about her sadness any more. But she told Annie, very gently and without any awkwardness, which was what made it so helpful, that Annie was going to be a beautiful woman now, a specially beautiful woman, and that Mrs. Hutchins was delighted to see how her body was beginning to change. And she would mention it to Annie in little ways occasionally after that, and it came to be a kind of special secret between them.

It wasn't until she was sixteen that Annie was able to be home at fish camping time again.

She was fully a woman in her body by then, and when she walked out into the warm clear water of the shallows she was suddenly terrified. For the magic the child had remembered so preciously wasn't there any more; and because it was not there, when she had counted so long and so much on the moment when she would be free for it again, she was wildly afraid that all that she had left behind and treasured in the secret places of her mind and had remembered through all the years among strangers, was not there any longer, and she would never, in all her life, find it again.

She turned and ran back to the camp to hold her mother while she cried—and the little ones, grandchildren now trekking with the old people and who hardly knew her, came to touch her for her sadness.

After the crying stopped, she took her mother and the little ones to swim with her, and when she saw the little ones splashing she began to delight in their small bodies shining in the wetness and the sun, and slowly her happiness came back to her.

They had only a little more than a week—Big Meadow did not stay out for long journeys and camps any more—but by the end of that time Annie had healed much of her sorrow. They spent long hours on the beach in the sun, and even her younger brother, who in his own time in the school had become very self-conscious of his body and quite unsure that it wasn't wrong for him to see his sisters without their clothing, finally joined them.

It was on the last day that Annie suddenly burst into uncontrollable laughter, but she dared not tell any of them what it was about.

It had suddenly come to her, with a profound sense of mischief in the thought, that her brother would die of embarrassment if, as he used to do, he should become erect, and the joke got even better when she thought that probably he was having to work very hard not to.

Annie never again lost her sense of the magic in bodies.

XXVI

Of course, the residential school and the hospital were both extremes of a sort, and when you tried to discover what it was that white people really felt about bodies, you had to look beyond those places.

But when you did it was confusing, and Annie found the confusion going about in her head as she took her weight on her feet in the stirrups to relieve the pounding of the brisk trot to which she pressed her horse. It was as though Gyp's mention of Petersen's obsession with cleanliness had brought up the whole puzzle again.

There was this great fuss about young women's bodies, but it was mainly a fuss about the particular beauty in young women's bodies that excites men in their sex.

Annie was glad that she had that special kind of beauty in her body, and she hoped she would have it for a long, long time. But it wasn't the only kind of beauty in bodies, and it seemed strange to fuss so much over that and then act as if there were no other kind of beauty in bodies at all.

No one seemed to know about the beauty in old bodies and large bodies and the new body of a baby lying on the old body of an aging parent.

You did not see white children playing naked in the sun.

And all the obsession with young women's bodies, with mainly the sexual quality in young women's bodies, was strange, too; for when you got down to it, white people didn't really seem to feel right about young women's bodies either.

There was this most fierce taboo against actually uncovering a woman completely. For a woman actually to be uncovered was, by all the evidence, an enormous sin.

But mostly people were busy seeing how far they could go without actually committing the sin. Bathing suits and daring dresses and pictures in advertisements were all part of this game of how far can you go without actually getting there. Probably that was a good thing, too, because if everybody actually respected the sin and stayed well away from it, nobody would ever see anything of young women's bodies at all, and that, Annie thought, would be a pity.

Some people were very rebellious and they actually committed the sin, but this was done in daring and was, therefore, awfully unnatural.

But how strange it all was. You could be sent to jail for being naked on a beach where people might see you, yet everyone seemed to think of nothing much else than what you would look like if you were naked.

It had something to do with the fact that white people really felt that there was something wrong with sex.

Of course, if you asked them they would all say that there was nothing wrong with sex and they would probably say how, after all, it was really very *natural*. But they had so many rules about it—which most of them wanted to break much of the time anyway—that it was plain they felt that something was wrong about it all.

If something is really good in every way, you don't have to have a bookful of rules about it.

And they seemed to think, at least the men seemed to think, that your sex was something that you could separate from all the rest of you—from how you felt and what you believed and who you were—so that you could make love without meaning it.

At the vocational school and while she had worked for a year, white men had taken a great interest in Annie. It had been flattering at first. But then she had found that she could hardly talk with any of these white men, for she never felt confident that they would understand her feelings, and none of them ever seemed concerned to try to give her that confidence.

In fact, all they really seemed to want to do was make love with her, and it did not matter to them that they did not know how she felt about anything, much less about that.

It angered her, because she wanted to make love, too. She wanted to make love as desperately and urgently as everyone does, and she ached with the wanting, especially in the treasured sense of how beautiful her body was in its promise of excitement and pleasure.

But making love was the most special kind of knowing; and you could not do it with someone who did not care who you were, who did not want to know the Annie who had delighted in her own child's body in the shallow water of the lakeshore at the fish camp with her family.

And she made this simple yardstick for the measuring of these men: she would ask herself while one of them made his terribly transparent approaches if he would go with her to the fish camp and enjoy her old father, if he would understand the comfort that little children found in the large folds of flesh that enclosed her mother, a body that to white people must be virtually obscene.

One by one, she would not see these men any more.

And whenever Annie tried to puzzle out these contradictions in how white people acted about bodies and sex, she wondered if it all had something to do with their religions, but it was hard for her to be sure. Most of them didn't subscribe to their religions any more, and all Annie knew of religion was what she knew of the Catholic religion, and that really didn't amount to much.

It was strange about being a Catholic, and she wondered if the priest really had any idea of what the people truly believed of it all. She'd heard him say in despair once that he didn't think there was a true Catholic among them, and Annie thought that probably he was right that time.

There wasn't any doubt that the rituals and customs of the Church had become part of the people's life. They'd go to mass and they'd go to confession and they'd go through all the movements and say all the words, and whenever the priest asked them anything, they'd tell him what he wanted to hear.

But it was all rather like Annie in her last year or two in the hospital, and at the vocational school, and when she'd worked for a year as a nurse's aide. She'd been at it so long she'd learned how to talk like a white person, to dress like a white person, to eat like a white person, to act like a white person in a house or at school or in a store or on a job.

She knew she'd done it well, far better than most Indian people ever can, and she had entirely fooled the white people around her. They thought she had become one of them—except for her dark skin, which they never quite forgot, even though they pretended they had—but how little they knew how unreal it was for her, all that acting like a white person.

It was like that with the religion. The people knew all the motions and they knew all the words, but did they believe in it? Annie didn't, and in fact, apart from the time in the school, she hadn't spent much of her life going through the motions. Her father had always resisted going through the motions, although under pressure from the priest he would go to church once in every long while.

And so when it came to accounting for the contradictions in how white people acted about bodies and sex, Annie understood too little of white religions to say what they really had to do with it, except that both the attitudes and the religions seemed some way sadly preoccupied with an ancient, inherited sense of sin.

Annie could not say, either, where her own people stood in the confusion; for it seemed, as the generations went by, that they were taking on the worst of what white people were, and were losing, at the same time, much of the best of themselves.

And so it had to be admitted that many of her own people had a sense of shame about bodies and guilt about sex, and that many of the men sought no meaning nor gave it in their lovemaking.

She did not know, either, what it had been like in the lost time before the white men had come. Perhaps the people had had their own illogical and depriving taboos, and she did know from the older women that they believed the tribe had always treated women harshly.

Annie wanted to believe that long ago the families had been like her family, unashamed and delighted in what they were, but she had no way to be sure.

Still, she treasured the wish.

And mostly when Annie could not make sense of white people and puzzled on them, it was this contradiction between what she found in them and what she had learned in those happy early years of her own life—the delight in bodies and the excitement they contained—that caught her imagination and fed the puzzling.

They were other things to puzzle on, if you cared to.

You could puzzle on why a white girl who had seemed to be your friend in the vocational school did not know you any more when unexpectedly some people from the town where she lived came to see her in the students' lounge.

You could puzzle on why, when you had telephoned to be sure that a small apartment that would be just right for you and that you could afford was still vacant, it was not vacant any longer when the landlady, with ill-concealed surprise, actually met you in person a five-minute taxi ride later.

You could puzzle on why, when you had gone alone to eat at an expensive restaurant as a diversion in your loneliness, three different white couples who had come in after you had been seated first.

And you could puzzle, if you liked, on why, no matter how hard you tried to live up to the expectations—to be punctual and hard-working at your job, to dress your best and be spotlessly clean, to pay your rent and live quietly beyond any reasonable point, to offer unfailing loyalty even to your briefest acquaintances, not to mention those you hoped you might call your friends—the fact that you were an Indian assured

135

you before you even started that it would not be enough when you were done.

But that was not worth puzzling on, for that was hardly a puzzle at all. That was just the endless reality that whiteness had always conveyed to you in your Indianness and with such subtle consistency that you really could not remember when you had first become conscious of it.

Annie dealt with it by denying its validity, quietly, inside herself, where nobody knew.

But still it hurt, and perhaps it had been the hurt, more than anything, that finally had sent her home.

XXVII

Coming back to her family and her village with the intention of not leaving again had brought much peace to Annie, and she had been able to laugh again almost in the old way, the way that was unknowing and uncaring of white people and what they expected of Indians and of how endless it all was, that monumental expectation that you could never fully understand, much less live up to.

And the laughter was in the simple delights like the perception, that time at the lake, of her younger brother's anxiety not to be erect, and of the innocence of the little ones, still with the freedom not to care.

And it was in the mouths stained blue with eating the Saskatoon berries from the bushes on a hot afternoon, in the gentle teasing of a young woman whose pregnancy had begun to show, and in the way an old blind woman still made her garden, planting the seeds on her hands and knees, with her old fingers enjoying the moist earth as she followed the string that marked the row.

It was in a young mother trying without success to tickle her baby awake so that he would suck from her too-full breast, and her delight when a toddler, still fond of sucking, climbed on her lap to relieve the difficulty.

But as good as it was to be home again and to be herself again, the woman of almost twenty could not be free of longing in the way of the child before nine. She had seen the world and knew its burdens. She had seen into her own heart and knew its hungers.

And in one sense the village was confined. The men there she might find love with she had in some way left behind. She did not understand it, but she knew that her coming back was one thing, while the unraveling of herself to a place where these men of her own village could reach her was another, and quite beyond her to accomplish.

She had watched the happiness of a cousin who had just immersed herself in all the pleasures of a first love, and she wished she had never been away.

And then Gyp had come to Upper Meadow.

And she had so resented his coming there that she quite forgot the emptiness inside herself.

To begin with, Upper Meadow had been so long un-occupied that Big Meadow Charlie had begun to feel that though it wasn't a reserve, perhaps it wasn't any longer white man's ground, either. He had not yet felt so confident that he would cut the hay from it, but he had, with others, turned horses there to paw through the snow for the dried grass in the early part of the winters.

But Gyp's coming destroyed the hope that the injustice of long ago, when Upper Meadow had been excluded from the reserve, would in some way inherent in the long passage of time be adjusted, and the place come back to the people.

Big Meadow did not speak of it, he only made different provision for his horses in early winter and, by his example, led others to do the same. But Annie knew his heart and she was angry, not with him for his acquiescing, but that this was the way of Indians with white people, and somehow it never changed.

And as for Gyp himself, though he was clearly in an eligible age range, being perhaps five years Annie's senior, she had made up her mind that he was positively unattractive. It was true that he was lean and firm and strong in a slow-moving way and favorably tall, but nothing could overcome the sheer bad luck of his looks. Annie was far from afflicted with that obsession with even and uniform features that distorts the judgment of white people, but ugly is ugly if it lands there on a man's face in the irredeemable solidity with which it had for Gyp.

His jaw was too short and his nose too flat and his eyes too wide apart. His mouth was crooked and his cheeks misshapen and his brow protruded, and in all probability he'd have looked better with no ears at all than with the small, crinkled tops and the enormous slabs at the bottoms of the ones he had.

Annie had almost felt sorry for him, but she had made up her mind against it.

She had been too busy, as well, resenting the fact that Gyp kept calling on her father for help of one kind or another and that her father, in his endless amiability, would never refuse him.

Gyp needed help to find some horses to buy, and to know when it was best to drain the meadow so the sod would dry enough to put the mower onto it to cut the hay. He needed to be shown the bush country to the west where his cattle would range, and where to shoot a fat buck in the fall for meat. And if he needed actual hands to hire for some short while, to stack the hay and to go that first time to drive in the cows he'd bought at Springhouse, he needed Big Meadow to tell him who he ought to hire and what he ought to pay.

It wasn't that he was helpless; far from it. It was apparent to everyone, very soon, that Gyp was a ranch-raised man who knew how to buck out a bad horse and put up hay, to grow a patch of spuds or butcher a moose, to fix a wagon with a hewn-out timber and a roll of wire, to make a door of split pine slabs and hinge it on a cabin with pieces of rawhide.

It was just that for all the bits and pieces of advice that would make it easier to get started on Upper Meadow, on the place that would have been part of the reserve but for the trickery of a government surveyor, he had discovered that Big Meadow was an endless source. And so he used him, and Annie did not like it, not one small particle.

To make it worse, she saw her father, in his straightforward, simple way, investing this new relationship with the sheer gold of his capacity for friendship, and she did not know how to tell him what a danger it was to give this to a white man. Apart from the priest and the Indian Agent and the store-keeper at Lance Creek (who came, anyway, in fixed relation-ships that safeguarded against both the investment of pro-found friendship and the risk of its being badly used), Gyp was the only white man who had ever actually entered into a continuing association with Big Meadow, and of course Big Meadow had no way to know the hurt it would inevitably lead to.

Annie feared for her father, and she resented Gyp the more that he would secure his advantage over her father by accept-ing the largeness of his heart—though a little guardedly and very secretly she admitted to herself that it all seemed genuine enough.

Certainly they got along together well. She knew that her father had an irrepressible capacity to ignore the demands of responsibility whenever some lighter pursuit might call him—

he would gladly leave the hay in the windrows to get rained on rather than bunch it and stack it at once if the securing of this particular hay happened unexpectedly to conflict with an impromptu stampede at another reserve anywhere within a hundred miles—but she knew also that in the long run, in the total sum of what he did and how he used himself and the time the passing seasons gave him, his family and his livestock would fare well enough for their physical wants.

And they would have, besides, this incalculable wealth, that Big Meadow Charlie cared for them; and Annie understood that you could suffer a lot of shortages and still be far ahead of the game if you had that.

But you had to accept that sometimes when it seemed most necessary that Big Meadow tend to the hay or fix the fence or go to the store or fetch some meat from the hills before the salt barrel would be empty with tomorrow morning's breakfast, Big Meadow would unaccountably disappear on some whim of an adventure that had not a damned thing to do with any of these urgencies.

And it seemed that this man Gyp, with whom he had inadvisedly taken up, was just as bad or worse.

Gyp would show up one morning with no previous announcement but with his best horse under him and with his next best led behind under a substantial pack, and Big Meadow would join him, and you wouldn't see either of them for the next two weeks.

In their absence the hay could grow too ripe and the best of the summer's dry weather waste and the firewood in the shed run out—and if you were unkind enough to get down to what it was that they had been doing, you would find it was nothing more than that they shared a delusion that somewhere upstream of the old workings on Snyder Creek, three days' ride to the northeast, there is a mother lode of pure gold spewing nuggets the size of cow's eyes, if a man could only find it.

For this particular recurring venture they shared between them two short shovels and a rusty gold pan, and judging by the size of their camp outfit and the sacks of dried meat they sometimes brought home with them, the preservation of their illusion about the gold was more a matter of how nice it was to bugger off—Gyp's own expression, not Annie's—into the hills, than of any real expectation, even in their susceptible minds, of riches in the gravel.

Annie sometimes doubted that the gold pan ever saw the creek bed.

She found herself wishing that they would both take things a little more seriously. Even with the good-humored indulgence that Annie possessed toward the weakness of others, the irresponsibility of her father and Gyp in consort was a little too much to bear benignly. Of course, it was excusable for her father, because he was, after all, an old man, but Gyp ought to have known better.

And anyway, he was a white man, and if he was going to make anything of Upper Meadow he was certainly going to have to pull up his socks.

She didn't appreciate, either, the brand of humor Gyp had, seemingly, developed to deflect any attempt to make him account for himself. It was a dry sort of humor, used to make light of the irresponsibility of his nature, and Annie chose not to care for it.

She asked him outright on one occasion if he ever looked for work to do around his own place, he was spending so much time on these capers with her father.

He said hell, no, he never looked for work. He tripped over more of it than he could handle just getting out of sight of it every day without *looking* for the damned stuff.

Now, what could you do with a man like that?

But Annie had to admit that, like her father, Gyp did

manage in the course of the passing seasons to get enough feed up and to see his stock through and to keep his place in some kind of repair.

But she sure did find him annoying.

XXVIII

But although Big Meadow did seem to spend an inordinate amount of time with his newfound friend, it was a fact that he also made journeys with those of his family still enchanted enough with the old ways of the wagon trail and the fish camp to bother with it.

Annie, of course, always went on these short treks, which were the surviving vestiges of those whole long summers spent in enchanted wandering fifteen years earlier; but she went not only for the love of it but also because she genuinely worried for her aging father.

It was no small task to harness and hitch a team and load an outfit on a wagon, then ride it as it jounced its way over the now little-used trails, and have to make the camp and tend the horses and do all that work that is essential to a camp of numerous people.

And although she was willing, Annie's mother could no longer help with the heavier work, and none of the boys, save Little Boy, cared any more for the journeying. And Little Boy cared for the journeying simply because he stayed happily in the shelter of his family; but he needed more looking out for than he could give back in work done.

But although none of the older boys who might have shared the work chose to go, certainly the grandchildren loved to go, and so Annie went happily but anxiously as well, for a wagonload of small children made more than a handful for two old people and one young woman.

Big Meadow moved ever so slowly now, and the packing and the unpacking of the wagon took a long time, and the climbing up and down from the seat had grown very difficult; and if a horse made a sudden movement as Big Meadow bent to set the hobbles, he could not get quickly out of the way.

Annie knew that the one remaining means of travel he found agreeable was to ride his old and trusted saddle horse. He could still heave himself up, and once there, he was comfortable. And Annie did not, however much Gyp annoyed her, do him the discredit of doubting whether he did the work of the camp for them both when they traveled.

It was hard, in fact, to unravel her feelings: the hurt of the old man spending so much time with Gyp; the anger at Gyp over how much he had accepted her father's simple genuineness; the even more troubling anger with Gyp as it grew less plausible for her to remain angry for the reasons she had adopted; her sorrow that her family was the last of the families to truly love the wandering; and her regret that of her family only herself and Little Boy and her small nieces and nephews, to whom it was all a rapture of adventure, were the only ones now to go with the old people.

It was in the late summer of the third year after Gyp had come to Upper Meadow that Big Meadow had the accident.

They had done their little haying with some help from the older boys and had then set off for the fish camp, where they wouldn't do any fishing that late in the season, but would swim in the shallows of the lake and enjoy lying on the beach in the last hot days of summer. Five little grandchildren clustered on the wagon with Little Boy and the old people, and Annie came behind on the saddle horse.

The trail on the first day led through timbered country that rolled in a gentle plateau to the southwestward; but it was obstructed now in places, and rather than undertake the heavy task of cutting out the windfallen timber, Big Meadow managed to work his way around and through the trees by the most expert driving of the team, sometimes swinging the horses and backing the wagon to put it at the precise angle to the spaces between the trees that would let it through.

Annie watched the wagon passing with sometimes no more than an inch to spare and with the horses' very noses crowded against an obstructing tree ahead before they were allowed to turn to avoid it, Big Meadow carefully not turning the wagon too soon, to avoid binding it in the narrow passage; and she sensed the long years that those old hands had held the mouths of horses in the gathered leather driving lines, and the long years that the eyes had visualized the wagon's width between the trees and known to that fraction that it would just go, given no less, not one hand span less of room ahead to put the team, before they must move to the left or the right of the next obstructing tree.

And so they made their way, slowly. And that night they drew up to camp at a small clearing by a stream where there was feed for the horses in the long pine grass under the trees.

Annie was unloading gear from the wagon with the intention of laying the tent out and perhaps getting it up, using the old poles left handy from previous camps made at that same place. She was thinking that if she managed this there would be less for her father to do when he was done hobbling the horses, when she heard the crashing of a horse lunging and the one sharp cry of pain from Big Meadow.

Annie dropped the bundle of bedding and for one brief part of a second she stood frozen, caught in the fear that the worst of all meanings was the inevitable meaning of that violent crashing and the one loud cry of pain, then silence.

Then her own brief cry tore her loose from where she stood, and she ran, wildly, into the timber. There she came on one horse hobbled and the other with a hobble half fixed and the halter rope dangling, eyes wide and staring in fright at the still figure of her father on his back beside a windfall.

She knelt, and as she knelt she saw in his face the struggle with pain, and she shook with the relief of knowing he was alive, and then with the grief of seeing so much pain in that so much loved face.

And she said inside herself O God, how badly, but to him she directed only the inquiry of her eyes, for he would tell her when he could, and she knew that she must not try to help him until he did.

Through the clenching against the pain he said first: "Catch that horse."

Which she did, easily, while the frightened beast stood trembling in his own evident confusion. She tied the halter shank around the nearest slender jack pine.

Then she knelt again to wait for what her father could tell her, and slowly now he managed it: "That horse, something scares him. He don't mean to knock me. I turn my foot when I go down." And he indicated his right leg with a slight movement of his hand.

Annie unlaced and removed the boot at once, working as quickly as she could while still being gentle. Bits of stored-up information from first-aid classes came to her mind, and she weighed the choice between making him as comfortable as she could where he lay or moving him somehow to the camp.

He must have been weighing it too. "In a little while, I make it to camp."

Annie could see the swelling starting to rise. "You can't tell if it's sprained or broken."

They thought about that, and while they did Annie realized that her mother had come as well, and had probably been there almost as soon as she had, but had left the dealing with it in her hands.

And Annie spared a moment to think of Little Boy and the fear that already would have taken hold of him and set him to the helpless trembling that marked his too-frequent fears; but she knew, too, that his needing comfort would keep, would have to keep, until she had done what she could for Big Meadow.

Big Meadow reached a decision: "You get on one side and your mum on the other. I can just make it. If I wait it's gettin' worse."

And thus they just did it, Big Meadow keeping the injured ankle up, moving the good foot ahead in short hops while he put his weight on the others.

They let him down to the ground beside the fire, and he lay out on his back to wait.

Annie and her mother then took the time for Little Boy. They stood with him, and held him, and spoke to him in reassuring words that Annie wished she might truly believe herself. And in a little while his fear lessened, and he stopped the transfixed staring at his father that in itself frightened Annie, for it revealed so profound a dependence that Big Meadow's life, all their lives, seemed suddenly fragile.

Then Annie set the tent and rolled out Big Meadow's bedding and helped him as he dragged himself onto it; and in the helping and the apprehensive watching of his face as the movement increased the pain she understood that it was no turned ankle that would mend itself by morning.

They were in trouble.

She hobbled the remaining work horse and the saddle horse as well, but later she changed the saddle horse to a long tether in the clearing. And she thought of the tortuous deserted trail back to Big Meadow and the narrow places where if you did not have the skill to maneuver the wagon you were bound to jam it in the attempt to get it through or, worse yet, panic the horses and damage the rig.

And if the ankle was broken, what a long, hard way that put them from getting it to help.

The pain grew worse and the cold cloths laid over it helped only a little. Just before dark Big Meadow called Annie to his side to tell her quietly of his own fears and what she must do.

"Maybe he's broken."

"You can't be sure."

"I never have hurt so much."

She took his hand and lowered her face to press the hand against her cheek, and he must have felt the tears there, for he squeezed her small hand with his huge one in response.

Then he said: "When daylight comes, you ride for Gyp."

And she thought, why Gyp, why not one of our own people, but she would not speak of it, she only moved away to fix a bed for herself so that she could rest before morning.

She left at daybreak, and when she had knelt again by Big Meadow before leaving it was to see that he had not slept in the night and that a trace of fear had joined the pain that was evident in his eyes.

It had been the trace of fear in Gyp's eyes when she had told him that had shot her through with shame and made her see that she had misjudged him.

She had found him, ax in hand, making rails to renew his stack yard fence, and he had stopped at once when he saw the lather on her horse.

She had said: "It's my dad. He's hurt."

And she might have cut him unexpectedly with a knife, for he visibly flinched and his face drained of color; and in that instant she knew she had used his own defensive front of indifferent smart remarks to deny his feeling.

She had scorned others because they could never have cared for her father, and then had refused to see that this one strange and solitary man loved him in a way that was utterly indifferent to the irrelevancies of their skin—both of his skin

147

and of her father's—though he was as inarticulate in his cloaking up of feeling behind his damnable silly jokes as she was in her shrinking away from that wash of white numbness that had all but drowned her in her years of trying to stay alive in it.

He asked: "What happened?"

"He turned his ankle. I think he broke it. I'm sure he broke it. He can't walk, and we got to get him out."

He dropped his ax and ran half the length of the meadow to his cabin, where in an unbelievably short few minutes he saddled his own horse, stripped Annie's rig from her horse and strapped it to a fresh one, then offered Annie cold grub in the cabin while he fetched a bottle of brandy from the cellar and rolled it into some blankets which, with his light jacket, he tied behind his saddle. Annie had to run from corral to cabin to corral to keep up with him, and before she had caught her breath they were striking out at a hard, persistent trot.

During all that fast journey back, which went into the dark of night before it brought them to the camp where Big Meadow lay injured, she wished that there was some way to say to Gyp that she had been wrong.

But she did not know whether she could make the words for it; nor was was there any opportunity for it, because Gyp did not once turn his face from the trail ahead.

XXIX

Within the small circle of light made by the candle against the surrounding darkness of the camp and the forest, Annie watched intently the faces of the two men, and in her father's face she saw that the pain, accumulating through the long hours in which he had not been able to sleep, was terrible.

But it reflected also his relief that they had arrived, that Gyp had arrived; and the old face, through the pain, made not a smile really but a faint bit of a laugh, and the old man said: "Maybe you best cut it off."

To which Gyp replied: "Yeh. I brought my knife. I'll cut it off at your crotch."

"You watch out your knife don't slip. You might spoil good stud." And the face managed a little more of the laugh that it could not make fully because of the pain; and Annie saw the slight movement in which, just for a moment, each man's hand found the other and gripped together.

Then Gyp fetched his small bedroll, and from out of it he took the brandy. Removing the cap from the bottle, he handed it to Big Meadow. The old man propped on an elbow and drank, and Gyp's tanned and stubbled face in the candle-light grinned its satisfaction as Big Meadow swallowed, coughing with the awkwardness, then grimaced in reaction to the strong bite of the undiluted drink.

"Enough?"

"Yeh. We make him last."

And with the brandy, and the lifting of his anxiety for those who depended on him, Big Meadow slept.

Gyp unsaddled and hobbled the two horses, then took his bedroll around the fire from the tent. A few embers still glowed in the ashes, and sitting on the bedroll, he made the fire up into a fresh blaze, then sat motionless, staring into the flames.

Annie had made a place with her blankets in the tent by her mother, but through the open flap of the tent she had watched Gyp's movements and then his face across the fire as the changing light from the flames made movements in the shadows around him; and with a quick resolve she rose and went to where he sat, kneeling on his bedding beside him.

"Gyp."

"Yeh."

"I'm sorry."

He turned to look at her, and under the looking she fixed her eyes into the fire. She wanted badly to meet his eyes, but she had exposed herself in those two words in a way she had not before, and there was no courage left for the touching of eyes.

He asked: "What for?"

And it was so simply asked that it bared his whole innocence, and his innocence so confounded her that she almost panicked with it. She forced herself not to get up and run away to the seclusion of the tent.

She forced herself to say: "Because I didn't like you."

His eyes turned back to the fire and she was able to watch him again, and for a long while he was quiet. Then he said: "I didn't know you didn't like me. But it wouldn't matter. Nothing says you got to like me. It's nice if someone likes you, but it isn't something a man's got any right to expect."

And she cried out inside herself that he was *wrong*, that he had every right, that they all had this right, and he had the right as well to be understood and known for what he was, and that he mattered.

And frantically she wanted to hit him with her fists and make him angry for this right; and the fury of her protestation built up inside her, driven by all the lonely, frightened years of her own not being known, and in the most terrible and unanswerable argument, the words in silence said themselves: *Even Indians got that right.*

But she could say nothing, and she cried quietly, kneeling before the fire, for what the not knowing world had done to her and to Gyp, and for what she had done to Gyp in her not knowing, and for his not even realizing it.

When she wiped the tears from her face with the back of

her hand, the wetness made the brown of her skin shine in the firelight.

Gyp said: "I'm sorry."

She said: "It's all right."

Then after a while she went back to the tent and lay by her mother. She heard Gyp stirring as he set out his bedroll and lay on the ground, gathering his canvas and his blankets around himself against the cold of the fire dying away.

In her mind she stayed where he lay until finally she went to sleep.

XXX

Big Meadow was better in the morning for having slept, and though the pain had not lessened, he had more strength with which to bear it. He and Gyp, in an exchange of disrespectful remarks about each other, decided to save the brandy against the traveling and the need for sleep again that night.

They discussed the traveling with Annie who stuck by the point that if the ankle was broken badly—and this seemed likely—the sooner it got to a doctor the better, and if it waited too long it would be beyond fixing properly.

This took some persisting, because Big Meadow leaned heavily to the notion that if Gyp would just shoot a few deer for them all to eat and ration out the brandy for the night-times, they could stay where they were, and the ankle could set itself in whatever order it saw fit. It might be a little lumpy, but it would be usable enough in a month or so. But Annie's argument prevailed.

Gyp used the tent and all the bedding and the spring tops of some fir branches as well to make a deep, soft bed at the back end of the wagon. With a great deal of care he made everything else into a compact load forward, with enough seating space on top of it all for the children and their grandmother. With a horse each for Annie and Little Boy, Gyp was left with the small space forward of the load on the wagon, where he could stand for the driving of the team.

Finally, with poles and canvas, he made a stretcher and helped Big Meadow to move himself onto it.

Then the brandy. "Here, y'old bastard. Have a smash."

Big Meadow drank one large swallow, then passed it back. "Gee, you tight with you bottle."

"Never mind. You break your neck next time and I'll fetch you a whole case."

"Just soon as my foot is better."

Then with Annie and her mother anxiously following Gyp's careful directions, they all three lifted the stretcher across the back of the wagon and by inches turned it until Big Meadow lay in the softness that Gyp had prepared for him as protection against the movement of the wagon.

It was a slow journey back, and it was filled with anxieties for Annie as she watched her father tense against the pain that came with each lurching of the wagon, in spite of the bedding and of the brandy, which every hour or two Gyp stopped to administer.

Each time the wagon had to leave the obstructed trail to find passage through the trees, her eyes would move from the narrowness of the way to the man in whose hands now the horses' mouths and the wagon's passage were gathered in the driving lines, and she would find herself breathing erratically in time with the progress of the rig.

But even in her anxiety, there was a new awareness now of this man whose back she watched as he took them in his hands by careful inches at a time toward help for the injured ankle. It was an awareness largely felt, not thought, and in it the back was tall and strong and fit for worthy burdens.

Later in the day, when the heat of the afternoon sun penetrated the shade of the trees and with the constant movement brought sweat to wet his shirt and make it cling, Annie could see the shape of the hardened muscles beneath it, and in her mind her hands traced the movement and felt the strength.

They camped that night still some hours out, since Gyp dared not travel in the dark. But it was a makeshift camp, and it used as little of the canvas and bedding as possible, leaving most of it for Big Meadow so that he might stay where he lay.

They moved out again at daybreak after a breakfast cooked over a fire that was really too large for cooking, but welcome for its warmth against the chill of the time before the dawn.

They reached Big Meadow by midmorning, and Gyp rode at once to Lance Creek to telephone for an aircraft.

Within the day Big Meadow was in the hospital at Williams Lake and, as he told about it afterward, that doctor just shook the pieces into place so quick and fixed him up in that cast so easy that Gyp could have done it himself if he'd had the book.

And Gyp would have spared him some brandy while he did it.

XXXI

Annie had expected, with that absolute assurance that is the due of a young and beautiful woman, to secure for herself all that her heart had so long yearned for, now that it lay so plainly before her for the taking.

When Gyp would come to the village to see how her father's leg was feeling or to fetch in the larger share of some meat he had killed, she would, seeing him come, take a little extra care with her hair and put on a neatly ironed blouse above her jeans, even sometimes a specially pretty dress she had saved from the days when she had lived in town.

Annie knew how to make the most of her black hair and large dark eyes and the soft curves of her slender body, and all in an unpretentious way. She had known men to stop in their tracks on the street to follow her with their eyes as proof of it.

And she was warm with Gyp now in small ways, without being forward about it. She would chat a little while she made and served him tea, and she would walk out of the cabin with him to thank him again if he'd brought meat or some vegetables from his garden.

Often he would come in the evening, and it would be dark when he would leave. Then she would go with him to her father's barn where his horse was tied if he had ridden in, or she would walk almost the whole way to Upper Meadow with him if he had come the three quarters of a mile on foot.

And she grew puzzled, for he did nothing.

He seemed to enjoy her friendly new ways, and he would talk with her in the little bits of nothing important between comfortable silences that were amiable to them both, but he wouldn't do anything.

Any other man she'd ever spent a quarter as much time with would long since have tried to take her to bed, but not, dammit, Gyp.

When she would walk with him that little way in the evenings and the time would come to say goodnight, she would stand close to him with her face turned up to his, her lips moist and slightly parted in anticipation, and wait.

But all he would do was offer his cheery good night and leave.

It really was too much. She had waited so long and patiently for the right man, and now to have him apparently oblivious to an opportunity that any other man on earth would have leaped at in a fever of desire was just painfully ridiculous.

She did not intend to put up with this foolishness.

She would give him one more chance.

By good luck her father asked her, the same afternoon that she had made this resolve, to take Gyp a box of cartridges for his carbine. Gyp had run short, and Big Meadow had promised to send some as soon as he collected the box he was owed by his brother-in-law, who was too blind now to shoot straight anyway. Many small transactions and several obligations to the brother-in-law in numerous cabins in the village resulted in the assembling of one full box of the correct caliber, and Annie delivered them.

When she did so, she tidied Gyp's table and straightened out the top of his stove and stepped up his fire and cleaned out his kettle, then put it on for tea. Then she dumped out the tea leaves of the last tea he had made, and put out a few biscuits of her own making that she had brought with her and reheated in Gyp's oven.

They had tea.

It was a quiet, congenial tea. They said nothing in that amiable way that had developed between them, and when Annie would look at him and smile demurely, even seductively, she thought, he would smile back in his unserious way and have another noisy gulp of tea.

What could you do with a man like that?

She was wearing a pretty orange dress that made the brown of her skin soar in rich contrast. She had known men to breathe heavily and flush with a runaway pulse when she

155

had walked by in it, far less sit just across the table where, in the provocative cut of the bodice, that little bare touch of the swell of her breast could be seen.

Gyp seemed totally unaware, and it occurred to her that if she proceeded then and there to take the dress off, he would probably go on drinking his tea.

It annoyed her. She didn't want to seduce him, she wanted him to seduce her, but by the look of things neither had the least hope of coming to pass.

There was nothing left for it. In one of those rare acts of sheer resolve of which she knew she was capable but in which she rarely indulged, she did the final precipitous thing.

She came back to his cabin late that evening, and without a word of explanation—what could you possibly explain to this impossible man that would be of the least use?—she made love to him.

And though it had left her gasping for breath when it was over—it had been delicious and consuming beyond even the expectations of her imagination—she retained enough consciousness to know that it had been a total and breathtaking surprise to Gyp.

She could not resist it—as they lay clinging together in the moist and cosy afterglow, she whispered in his ear: "Why did it take you so long to do that?"

And whether he was, in fact, deluded by the event as to who had done the doing and to whom, or was merely unable to cope with a joke in that moment, Annie could not tell and did not care to pursue; for the answer he made was so pathetic to her, that if she had said any more she would have cried.

He had said: "I never thought a woman could want me."

And the worst of it, the crying pity of it, was the matter-of-factness of the saying, the simple belief that being not wanted was being Gyp Sandhouse, and not therefore any cause for despair or anger or grief or crying out against.

She held him tightly, her face pressed against him, into the strong man smell of his skin.

XXXII

Then Gyp did that incredible thing that was beyond any reasonable expectation.

He wouldn't let Annie live with him, and he wouldn't let babies result from their lovemaking.

Neither did he care to talk about it, and Annie, hurt rather than angry, only pressed the matter once and then just gently.

Making love, she explained, wasn't something you did all by itself, it was part of two people sharing their lives; and so it meant her looking after his cabin and washing his clothes and having his children and, for that matter, sharing his bad luck—his summers that were too wet for haying and his winters that were too long for feeding, and all the other uncomplicated misfortunes of his simple existence.

But it was no use. Whatever the fears were that prevented his accepting what love offered, he kept them secret, perhaps even from himself. And so, in the result, he divided their lives into the compartments of night and day, and he preserved their separation with a persistence that would have been cruel if Annie had not had the compassion of her love with which to endure it.

In the nights they loved in a free and uncomplicated way that left Annie floating on clouds of pleasure and fulfillment. She had grown up with an ever-present belief, founded not in any rational argument to which she gave words, but implicitly in how good her body felt, that the ultimate experience would be the sexual one—even Sister Mary had not dented this foundation for joy—and now, in the realization, there was only wonder for how much more was in the fulfillment than the anticipation.

Annie lived expressly to love. To love, to make love, with Gyp, was beautiful, and she never doubted it was as beautiful for him as for her. Repeatedly, she drove him wild with sensation, then left him exhausted with its ultimate explosion.

Then there was the damned silly business of the days in which this impossible man would act as if Annie were no part of his life. He would visit her father and accept the tea she served as though she were no different from any one of a dozen others in the house who might have waited on him, as they would on any visitor.

And when she could no longer bear the inadequacy of his housekeeping in the cabin that by night was as much hers as his, and began returning to it in the daytime while he was out to make it the clean yet casual place that was fit, in Annie's opinion, for any kind of sane living, he carefully did not notice the difference.

But she loved him, and she was not angry. She knew the gift of love she was, and if he could not for these obscure reasons accept it all, she could only be sorry for his loss.

And sorry for her loss, too. For she wanted to share his life and to have his children, and the resentment that accumulated in her was against not Gyp but whatever it was in him that deprived them both of what so naturally they ought to have.

And that resentment did accumulate until finally there were times when she felt ready to explode with it; but she was never sure in what direction: against men for their irresponsibility, or white people for their sexual confusion, or the world in general on account of the complication of everybody's lives with different colors of skin, or her own frustration at not knowing what it was in Gyp that made him such a contradiction.

So, divided into beautiful nights and puzzling days, their lives went on, and nothing much of a momentous nature interrupted the course of things until Moses Crease began to go wild again and Little Boy inadvertently killed him.

Then, strangely, there was all this upheaval that was so terrible in some ways and so funny it made your sides ache in others and stirred them all up like a horse stepping into a hornet's nest, and there was no telling how it would all end.

And, Annie mused to herself as Upper Meadow came into sight, if this prude of a white man thinks that he can look down on Gyp because Gyp lives with *this* Indian woman, even part time, then he's got another think coming.

So he wants a bath. He wants to be clean again so he can be the big white authority again.

Well, he'll get his bath.

And maybe he'll get the nightmare Gyp thought might make him want to forget it all and leave Gyp alone.

Annie had not looked forward to any diversion so much in ages.

XXXIII

Petersen was an orderly person, but then he had had very orderly parents.

His father had worked diligently for the Canadian Pacific Railway and had risen to a not inconsiderable position in the administrative offices in Winnipeg. Working for the railway was the only job he had ever held. He had begun it at seventeen and retired from it at sixty-five, and he used to say things like life is too short to waste it jumping from one job to another and if a thing is worth doing it is worth doing properly and I don't mind what you do for a living, son, but do it well and a penny saved is a penny earned, and all kinds of similar things too numerous to mention.

He also said that an orderly desk demonstrated an orderly mind, and so the office he set off to in his neat blue business suit freshly pressed at twenty-five of eight through the forty-eight years of his service was as impeccably neat a domain as the house he set off from for almost as many years.

And that house that he set off from was an unpretentious and well-kept little house in the suburbs that his wife devoted herself to so entirely that it was hard to tell whether she kept the house for the benefit of the people in it, or the people in it for the benefit of the house.

It was spotless, and the younger Petersen, born into it, was kept spotless too, and his socks were picked up after him and his bed made and his shirts ironed and his clean underwear laid out for him, in all that same grand orderliness that supported his father's passage through life in blue business suits impeccably pressed.

And Petersen did well at school, very well in fact, for his father said things like spare the rod and spoil the child and busy hands have no time for mischief and a little discipline is what they need, and so had arranged his son's attendance at a private school run on military lines where a great number of things were said similar to his father's sayings, and about as original.

Petersen had thrived in this setting, for the next best thing to having his mother keep him clean and tidy was an imposed discipline that gave him no alternative but to do these things for himself. He was a model student, and he made an excellent prefect.

It had not been at all surprising, as the continued order-liness of his life unfolded in the expected ways, that, having chosen a career in the Royal Canadian Mounted Police—he wanted to do something just a little more exciting than being an administrator for the CPR—he had stood at the head of his class at the training camp in Regina.

It had all come so easily to him—the rigorous physical train-ing, the tightly kept schedule of daily activities, the system-atic demands on, in his case, an orderly and well-disciplined intelligence—that he had found it difficult to have much sym-pathy for many of the others who found it almost impossible to keep up the pace.

He had been made corporal and then sergeant much younger than most men, and he looked forward, in the proper order of things, to becoming an inspector, a rare and much exalted post in the Force.

He had married, but only after he had become corporal, had established a reputation throughout the division as a serious policeman, and had saved, from his salary, quite enough to make most of the purchase price of a house. He knew it was very conservative to want to avoid a large mort-gage, but he saw no point in paying all that interest. In any case, he saw nothing wrong with a basically conservative turn of mind. He knew he was of that disposition, but it had clearly served him well.

He had married sensibly, of course. Mind you, he had chosen a good-looking girl. After all, he knew himself to be handsome enough, and it was only appropriate that he marry a woman equal of him in this sense; but apart from that, he disliked women who were not firm and well kept and likely to stay that way, finding those on the large side to be posi-tively repulsive.

But as well he had chosen an intelligent woman with all the good, conventional virtues—hard-working, thrifty, committed to tidiness, gracious, and, of course, with a perfectly protected reputation and the good sense to keep it that way.

They had both been virgins when they married, and Petersen could be thoroughly assured that, in her case, there had never been let happen even a circumstance in which any threat to that condition might have occurred.

For himself there was just one blemish. He had, on one occasion, on a date with a very warm and attractive woman, been carried away by his passions. They had been on a beach on a hot evening after a dance and he had attempted intimacies that would have led to everything if she had not stopped him in time.

She had been very nice with him about it, but he wished afterward that she had had better sense than to have let them get into such a situation to start with—if she'd thought of her reputation she'd not have suggested they walk on the beach in the first place—and he avoided going out with her again.

Of course, his marriage was very successful, and he never looked at another woman. He had very early established a pattern for their lovemaking that was entirely satisfying to him, and it had remained, without any blemish or necessity to change, entirely satisfying through the years of their life together.

He liked to make his advances on nights when he didn't have an early shift in the morning, and it had been a simple matter to discourage her from making initiatives of her own at other times—or at all, for that matter, as he believed firmly in the man being, logically, the dominant partner. And logically it was the man who caressed the woman and not the woman the man. There were some things that were self-evident, and he would not have tolerated any forwardness that went against them.

There had been just a couple of times—once when she had tried to get him to experiment with some odd position that

he really felt was a little improper, and another when she had
wanted them to actually take a shower together—that he had
had to disappoint her, but those were minor occurrences almost forgotten now as he looked back over fifteen years of
wedded happiness neatly integrated with the orderly progress
of his career in the RCMP.

XXXIV

But Petersen's orderly life in the RCMP had never wit-
nessed such chaos as it had been forced to endure in this
damnable business of Little Boy and Big Meadow and Gyp
Sandhouse. Not by a damned long way, and Petersen had
about exhausted himself with his own anger by the time he
set off from the camp to let the saddle horse take him back to
Sandhouse's cabin at Upper Meadow.

In fact, he had probably almost run the very last of his
equilibrium right out at the point when, in despair of ac-
complishing anything in the quagmire of duplicity that surrounded him, he'd asked Sandhouse if there wasn't a bathtub
somewhere.

And there hadn't even been that.

He couldn't make out whether Sandhouse was plain stupid
or brilliantly conniving and, if either, for what conceivable
purpose. What could it possibly matter whether Little Boy
had to go to jail or not, weighed against the risk to Sandhouse of having to go to jail for the futile attempt to help
him evade custody?

Never in all of Petersen's career had a situation got so
completely out of his control and so persistently and infuri-

atingly stayed that way, in defiance of his attempts to get hold of it.

And now the final torturing twist had been added to the maddening elusiveness of any order at all in this snarl of ignorant maneuvering; given the innocence, so belatedly discovered by them both, of Little Boy's haphazard deed, Petersen's task of nailing Sandhouse to the wall for the realization of at least a fragment of justice had just become exceedingly difficult.

It had become exceedingly difficult because the law, whether in wisdom or not—and at this moment Petersen believed not—made an offense of the hiding of Little Boy only in the case of Little Boy himself actually being guilty of something.

Which, it had turned out, he wasn't.

That would have been solution enough in any ordinary case, a good reason for pursuing the matter no farther, for closing the file neatly perforce and being spared the detail of preparing and bringing a case before the court, a perfectly satisfactory result.

But not, dammit, this time.

Not this time, because this time, for the first time in all these years of conscious and deliberate impartiality in the performance of duty and the enforcement of law, of unruffled, impeccable objectivity and disdain for the least vindictive feeling, Petersen had succumbed to human failing—and he wanted to get Sandhouse so badly he could taste it.

Which brought Petersen squarely against the dilemma of dealing with guilt in Gyp's intent when there was, finally, no guilt in his deed by which to demonstrate guilt beyond any question or reasonable doubt.

The guilt in Gyp's intent was clear, deliciously clear to Petersen now that he had abandoned himself to the vindictiveness of his exploding frustration; for Gyp had assumed, as they all had assumed, that Little Boy was in deep trouble, and he had hidden him and he had led Shaw on a wild goose chase and he had ditched him and he had lied and denied and persisted in the hiding of Little Boy.

But unfortunately there exists that damned tedious uncertainty about just that kind of guilt, that guilt of intent, which does not result, finally, in precise, clear criminal deeds that you may parade before judges for the finding of guilt.

But Petersen would find a way.

He would find a way because this damnable Sandhouse, this small-time, come-to-nothing bush rancher who hadn't enough brains to come in out of the rain, had been making a fool of the law for a whole interminable week over absolutely nothing when you finally got down to it—and it was more than Petersen, in the person of the law that had been made a fool of, could stand any longer.

But he was tired now, and the long trip back to Upper Meadow had tired him even more. In his exhaustion, his frustration and his anger had given way to an overwhelming apathy, the like of which he had never before experienced.

He turned the horse loose in the yard on his arrival and went at once to the cabin where, failing to find some food he could eat without the bother of preparing it, he fell on the bed and tried to sleep. But even that did not come easily, and it was far into the night after the cold had made him drag some covers over himself that he finally went into a fitful sleep.

The next morning, late, he made a fire and found some rather aged root vegetables to cook but nothing else, and he could not face any more of the dried meat (or the salted meat from the brine barrel) that Sandhouse seemed to live on. Petersen half ate the meal, and then supposed he ought to clean up, but found the effort even of making a start too much, and lay again on the bed.

This time he slept quite easily and did not wake until nearly suppertime. He tried again to summon up the will to put together a reasonable meal. But once more he ended up eating a few boiled vegetables and drinking some tea and, with a slight feeling of disgust with himself, leaving the dishes in disarray on the table.

Somehow his will to maintain orderliness had been wrested from him, and as dirty and tired and desperate for a change of clothes as he was, there did not seem to be a shred of will in him to do the least thing about it.

He wished passionately to be at home where all the familiar cleanliness would take him back into its fold and turn him out so effortlessly, as it does every day, clean and closely shaved and in a fresh, sharply pressed uniform.

He sank into the large chair. He had no idea how long he had been sitting there when he heard the knock on the door and that bit of an Indian woman of Sandhouse's walked in.

XXXV

Annie had had the scheme quite thoroughly in mind long before she arrived, late, but still with an hour or two of daylight left, at Upper Meadow.

But she hadn't expected to find Sergeant Petersen in quite such complete disorder, and she enlarged the scheme at once to take total advantage of it.

She knocked on the cabin door, and he answered. She entered, and in a quick sweep of her eyes about the cabin she saw it all—the bed unmade—the dishes not washed, Petersen unshaven and sitting dejectedly in the large chair, his uniform soiled and rumpled.

She did not know where the resolve came from, for however strong-minded and self-directed she knew herself to be among her own people—and in that one presumptuous, capturing stroke of boldness with Gyp—she had never imagined herself so bold as to impose her will on a figure of white authority.

But she knew that now she must, for the scheme depended on it.

And certainly she knew how to go about it. She had seen ninety-pound nurses tell the tycoons of white power—bank managers and steel-jawed business executives—to wipe their chins and blow their noses. It was all a matter of having them out of their element and hitting them hard. And right now Petersen was right out of his element.

It wasn't in her nature, but she had acted like a white woman in other ways and she could manage this. The hardest part was talking so fast. You had to make words like cold water landing on a hot frying pan.

She lit into Petersen: "Look at this mess! Look at Gyp's cabin! Look at you! I never saw such a mess!"

She strode into the middle of the room. Petersen stared at her in amazement as she indicated it all with a sweep of her hand.

"Look at it! And you haven't shaved since you came here. Do you think we're all a bunch of uncivilized savages around here that you can act like this? What would your wife think? Oh! It's disgusting!"

"Well, I . . ."

"Oh, you white men. You're so useless when you don't have someone waiting on you all the time." And quickly Annie began raking about in the firebox of the stove with a poker, shaking down the ashes from the coals, preparatory to putting on fresh wood. She hoped Petersen wouldn't talk back, because her act so delighted her inside where she was making

167

it up as she went along that she wasn't sure she could say much more without laughing outright.

She was relieved that as she put wood on the fire, and set a kettle to heat, Petersen got quickly to his feet and began doing ineffectual things to tidy the top of the table.

Annie rounded up water buckets—she found four—and stopped Petersen from what he was doing by sending him to the creek to fill them. While he was occupied making the two trips needed to fetch them back full she made a little kindling to liven the fire and bring the stovetop to a fearful heat.

When Petersen brought the second pair of buckets she put all four on top of the stove, then instructed him further, but now her voice was not quite so severe. She had control, and she knew she wouldn't lose it. It had been a heady sensation, seeing this large policeman meekly carrying water buckets at her command, but she had no wish to overplay her hand.

"This kettle is nearly hot. Now you shave yourself and I'll be back with a washtub by the time these buckets are ready. Goodness! Do *you* ever need a bath!" And she made a little sign with her nose that indicated a rather bad smell, then left.

Petersen, dumfounded, fetched his kit and began to shave.

XXXVI

Petersen shaved with the hot water in the tin hand basin on the stand by the door, watching himself as he did so in the small piece of broken mirror that was held by bent nails to the log by the door frame.

Damn, he thought, as he took long, careful swipes with the razor, I would never have guessed that that little Indian woman had it in her. Must have been out to a school or something. They would never be that assertive on their own, these Indian women.

And he very secretly admitted to being just a little ashamed that she had found him as she had. Apart from the guilt it had awakened in his memory from the times when his mother shamed him for some small but offending untidiness, he knew it was very eroding to his authority to let her have ground from which to assume the right to berate him like that.

But he'd soon put her back in her place. In fact, he'd be just a little deliberately more firm than was his usual way when she returned with that tub—just in case she'd got any idea that she had the upper hand after that rather improper business earlier.

But Petersen's resolve did him precious little good when, some time after he had done shaving, Annie returned.

It did him precious little good because when Annie returned, she returned not only with an incredibly inadequate-looking galvanized tin tub no more than about two feet by two feet that you could hardly imagine sitting down in no matter how you scrunched yourself together, but also with half a dozen older women from the village, substantial older women, every solitary one of them as immense as old Big Meadow Charlie himself.

And they paid him not the least attention. Not even Annie glanced in his direction. They just went directly to cleaning up that cabin like a squad of giant bees. They made the bed and swept the floor and cleaned the table and, with sparing use of water, washed the dishes and restored them to the makeshift cupboard.

Petersen had to look lively to get out of the way of one who, sweeping the floor, swept right into his feet as if he weren't there, and then jump from the way of another who, making the bed, was moving in ponderous but highly deter-mined journeys up and down the length of it.

The little cabin was full of them, these strangely deter-mined and enormous bustling women, and they so ignored him that not being run over became a serious and difficult prob-lem; in constantly dealing with it, Petersen's sense of in-significance mounted with every inept leap out of the way of one and into the way of another.

They went far beyond the disarray that could be credited to Petersen's short stay. They tidied shelves and poked into corners and gathered up bits of Gyp's clothing that lay about, and Annie even went into drawers to take out clothing that looked to have been not too badly folded at one time and put away there.

Within half an hour, half an hour in which Petersen felt reduced to the status of a mouse caught in heavy traffic at an unlighted intersection, they had made that cabin over into a model display of frontier housekeeping.

And Annie had been constantly feeding small sticks to the fire until now the buckets were steaming.

Then, all the activity ceased. That preposterous tub, that most inane instrument of ablution, surely only useful for those cartoons of ridiculous red-nosed men having caught cold being obliged by their wives to soak their feet in hot water, that thing was set squarely in the center of the floor and Annie fetched the buckets of hot water and spilled them in.

Then Annie looked at him and spoke: "Now you are going to have a bath."

Petersen viewed the tub with apprehension. He said: "Yes. I imagine one can. Somehow." And he waited for them to leave.

But they did not leave.

They did not leave at all.

Instead, they converged on him.

They converged on him, every one of them but Annie, and twelve strong, persistent hands began undoing the buckles and the buttons and the laces of his clothing, and his startled outcry of protest was drowned by the enormous giggling laughter that surrounded him.

He tried to push the hands away, but no sooner would he rescue a button from the attack of one pair of hands than another would be onto it, and while he was waging this losing battle over tunic buttons, the RCMP uniform was being totally overrun elsewhere.

One by one, the garments went—boots, trousers, tunic, shirt, and then, just pause enough for the horror of the inevitability to numb him, the last of everything.

He stood naked, totally exposed, as he had never been exposed.

His sources of strength were gone.

He stood dumb in humiliation, and the humiliation slowly turned to a kind of freezing terror at the realization of total helplessness.

He shivered in his nakedness before the surrounding enclosure of large, powerful women, and they only laughed. Here, in this insignificant cabin in the middle of nothing, they took away the means of what and who he was, and then they only laughed.

Then they grasped him, in all their hands at once it seemed, and moved him forcefully across the floor to the tub and made him step into the water.

Appalled, he resisted no more. But God help him, were they going to make him sit? In that impossible little tin tub?

But no, they let him stand, and now they fetched soap and, spilling water over him with a dipper, they began washing him with their hands.

The water was very hot, deliciously hot, and the women worked up a thick, creamy lather with the soap, and they began to cover him with it. Their fingers were strong and their hands were agile, and they took possession of Petersen's skin —which began with a startling upsurge of response to deliver its pleasure into his senses.

And every other reality in Petersen's consciousness left him, for his awareness was now filled with this pulsing sensation of hands on his skin, strong, sensuous hands, constantly moving.

His eyes closed and he swam in a kind of trance where he consisted no more of anything but his flesh, and it was on fire with a totally new pleasure, a pleasure he had not known existed.

And then into the trance, serpentlike, slithered the guilt, the strong, searing, ancestral guilt, for the pleasure, beyond telling, was sexual; and it was a sin, that pleasure, a sin of boundless proportions.

But Petersen could not help himself. He was without the physical strength to drive the hands away, and he was without the will to drive the pleasure away.

The guilt moved about, slithered about in the trance of exquisite pleasure, and it presented Petersen with the chaste image of his wife, smiling in the unspoken expectation of the fidelity both of his body and of his mind.

He cringed with the penetration of the guilt into this raw, exposed awareness where nothing now could be hidden, not now, not with his depravity laid bare in the rising crescendos of pleasure and excitement that were sweeping over him and rippling through his skin in pulsating waves.

He cringed, but he had nothing to offer in atonement or mitigation, nothing to abate the unspeakable offense against the self-righteous law that thou shalt not have pleasure save in thy narrow way and in only one place.

The hands had been all over his back and arms and chest and legs and stomach, and in another great paroxysm of guilt he knew that he was wishing the hands to go on and on, to run about his flesh, to drive him into the deliriums of ecstasy.

All his power of concentration fixed on that one consuming wish.

The guilt rose in concentrating surges until it seemed sure to destroy him in one final shattering burst, but still he could not abandon the pleasure wish.

His eyes closed, he stood faint in a sea of hot sensation that soaked deliciously into his flesh from where it rippled about his skin, and desperately he tried in silent willing to so direct the hands.

Annie poured the whole cold bucket of icy creek water down over him in one enormous, walloping splash.

He screamed and they laughed.

Annie tossed him a towel. "Here," she said. "Dry yourself."

Petersen, his own scream still ringing in his ears, stood naked in a cold and friendless place.

XXXVII

They did not even leave him alone to dry himself, and his nakedness made him feel that nobody knew who he was, that indeed he was not anybody, that even if he went where he had been known, he would not be known any more.

He did not belong. Not anywhere.

While he was drying, some of the women left with Annie. But two of them stayed, and they cleaned up the floor where the bath had been and stoked the stove and lit the lamp, and Petersen might not have been there for all that they noticed him.

He wondered where his clothing was, but could see it nowhere and did not have the courage to ask. He looked about for something of Sandhouse's. But he soon discovered that every kind of clothing of his was gone, too, even from the drawers of the old chest that sat against the wall at the end of the bed.

There was nothing.

He was nothing.

He got into the bed. It was the only place left, and after he was under the bedclothes he began to feel warm again, and then he realized that from somewhere Annie had produced clean flannelette sheets and that the bed was a very comforting place to be.

The flannelette felt good against his skin.

A long while later, he wasn't sure when, but he didn't think he'd been asleep, Annie came back. This time she had hot food with her in a large pot, and Petersen could smell it the moment she came in. It smelled deliciously appetizing, and he realized that he was very hungry.

She brought him a plateful to the bed with a spoon to eat with, and she waited quietly while he ate, sitting innocently on the edge of the bed at the foot.

The food was strange to him, but he couldn't remember ever enjoying anything so much. He wanted to ask what it was, but again found himself wanting for the little bit of courage to ask a simple question.

He realized that he had not known that Indian people had their own foods that were so different.

When he had finished the plateful Annie brought him more, and when he had finished that, he did muster the courage to ask about his clothes.

"Where's my uniform?"

"We're cleaning it. You'll get it back in the morning."

"Isn't there *something* I could wear?"

174

"You don't need anything till morning. You can stay in bed."

She didn't stay to see if he had anything to say to that, and Petersen couldn't be sure whether she was laughing at him or not.

The uncertainty made him miserable, and it was terrible to even care what that scrap of a girl thought of him, one way or the other.

But he did care and couldn't deny it.

He slept well, surprisingly enough, though it was the kind of sleep that is helped by a sense of defeat about one's fortunes.

When he awoke it was morning, and the women were coming and going from the cabin again. Their numbers varied but they had become ubiquitous, and Petersen wondered if he would ever be rid of them. But it occurred to him, too (oddly enough, he thought), that there was something rather attractive about them in their strange way. He wondered if when he spoke to one of them he'd get a reply, but he didn't put it to the test.

Then hot water was poured in the basin for him to wash with and shave, and a towel offered him to wrap around his middle, all wordlessly, and so he rose and complied.

Then they cooked him a large breakfast of hotcakes and bacon and eggs with coffee, and he began to feel himself again as he put it away, sitting at the table, still wrapped in his towel. Once he got his uniform back on, he felt he could be back to normal fairly soon, and able to get some reasonable grasp of his situation again.

But that speculation failed to account for several things.

It failed to account for the fact that it was much later than Petersen thought, that Shaw with his prisoners and his Indian scout had camped only a short way out the night before, and that they would arrive in a solemn procession before Petersen's uniform did.

In fact, as announced by one of the women in the first acknowledgment that any of them had so much as two words of English, Shaw and his party could be seen coming around the edge of the meadow even now.

XXXVIII

All of this accounted for the strange sight that greeted the arriving party—the sight of Petersen, black with rage, standing in front of the cabin and wrapped in a blanket in the fashion of a Plains Indian, his bare feet and white legs planted apart in a stance of defiance.

For suddenly, on the news of the impending arrival of the other men, strength and authority had returned to Petersen without even waiting for the return of his uniform. He had bolted to life and, wrapping the blanket over his shoulders and about his body, he had strode out the door to challenge the world.

He saw the party ride in, back from the long trail, in ceremonious procession, Big Meadow in the lead, followed by Little Boy and Gyp Sandhouse, and finally by Shaw—and damn Shaw if he wasn't shaved and somehow looking presentable as hell, and sitting upright in the saddle as if he owned the world.

Petersen glared into their eyes one by one, and it was a challenge to them all to be amused if they wished but, by God, they would do so at their peril.

Not an eyelid quivered.

Shaw dismounted, stood to attention before his blanketed superior, and saluted smartly. "Sir!"

"Yes."

"Your prisoners, sir."

Petersen glared at Shaw. The ass was in bliss in every make-believe shred of this colossal idiocy, and why, in God's name heaven preserve us, shouldn't he be? For the first time, though too late to really matter, Little Boy is, in fact, delivered in custody.

"Well, done, Shaw."

"Thank you, sir."

This drama was then interrupted by a great giggling from within the cabin. The cause of it was never fixed. Indeed, it would have occurred to none of the men there to pursue the cause of any laughter in all that abundant absurdity; they only were caught by the sound of it, and there was no ignoring it, for it was too substantial.

Petersen frowned as he looked from face to face, but expressions did not change.

Then in sudden resolve he spun on his feet, the blanket swirling out around him, and strode to the door, throwing it open.

"Get the hell out of here!" he bellowed, and in a procession one by one, all six huge women, tittering in their large, jelly-shaking fashion, trooped out and went off, still giggling, in the direction of the Big Meadow Reserve.

Petersen stood as though in inspection as they went by, and when the last had passed he took up his stance again before the assembled riders—and the standing Shaw, still firmly at attention—and once more met the eyes, chiefly of Big Meadow and Sandhouse, in furious defiance.

It was Big Meadow whose eyes twinkled unmistakably, whose face lit up in amusement, yes, but clearly also in admiration of a man whose prowess was indisputable and un-challengeable.

And Petersen found himself, strangely, not displeased with this acknowledgment; in fact, for some stupid reason he found it all just a little funny himself and he laughed a small laugh, a modest chuckle to show that he was, after all, a man of the world. But a man of authority as well, assuredly. In fact, a man of such authority that he could bear to be found here in all these wholly unusual circumstances without the least erosion of that authority.

There are few such men.

You come on them only rarely.

But it was time to reassert the authority.

He bellowed for the world to hear: "Where in bloody hell is my uniform!"

And this was a strange thing to bellow; for in all truth, Petersen had no idea or even cause to hope that Annie was any closer than the village, and it was an assured fact that no one else was going to produce his uniform.

But there she was just beside the cabin and where, evidently, she must have been standing all this time, just offstage.

Astounding little woman. Be a lively business to be married to her. Wouldn't mind it a bit, either.

And Annie came forward and handed Petersen his uniform, all spotlessly clean and sharply pressed, and his boots shining with fresh polish, found who knows where in this last of all places you'd expect to find shoe polish, and his underclothing impeccably white and folded.

She handed him them all, smiling sweetly, innocently, demurely, the very epitome of dutiful womanhood.

"Thank you. Thank you kindly," he said graciously, taking his clothing with one hand while he continued to clutch his blanket about himself with the other.

And then he looked at Shaw again, and Shaw had not so

much as quivered at the corners of his mouth. There was a lot to be said for a man like that. First-class control.

"Shaw."

"Yes, sir."

"Fine piece of police work you've done. You're a credit to the Force."

"Thank you, sir."

"I'll see you're commended for it."

"Thank you, sir."

"By the way, things aren't quite what they appear here."

"I understand, sir. It's just between us, sir. It's nothing you'd mention."

"Thank you. Now you'll have to excuse me while I change."

And when Petersen emerged again a few minutes later he felt splendidly fresh and well turned out and fit for the work at hand, to which he set himself at once.

He asked Big Meadow and Little Boy to come into the cabin together to give statements and gave Sandhouse leave to strip and feed the horses, detailing Shaw to lend him a hand.

XXXIX

Petersen's interview with Gyp was short.

They went alone into the cabin after statements had been taken from Big Meadow and Little Boy.

"Sandhouse." Petersen had that firm way about him again, but only firm, not iron hard. He sat upright at the table with his briefcase before him and all his papers stowed away within it.

Gyp sat on the edge of his bed, glad to be back to its comfort. He was also mildly surprised to see how tidy the cabin was. Clearly it had been through one of the sieges of house-cleaning to which Annie subjected it occasionally.

"Sandhouse, I don't need to explain to you again that Little Boy is not in any trouble. I've taken statements, and it's all plain enough."

Gyp said nothing. It wasn't his custom to comment on the obvious.

"Sandhouse."

"Yes."

"Do you very often come out to Williams Lake?"

"Twice in five years. I don't much care for the place."

"Would you do me a favor then? Would you so arrange your affairs that you do not come to Williams Lake *at all?*" The words were the kind of words that might have been said with some bite, some implication of the disaster to Petersen that Sandhouse had been, but oddly they weren't said that way at all. They were said almost imploringly.

Gyp said: "I thought I was going there whether I like it or not. As your guest."

"I have reconsidered that."

"Oh."

"I have decided that if I should tell a judge what has been going on here, in all its remarkable details, he wouldn't believe me for one minute."

"That's a possibility, Petersen. And I speak from experience, as you know. But you could give it the old try. He might believe *some* of it. I could help. I could tell him about . . ."

"Sandhouse."

"Yes."

"I don't want to hear what you would tell him about."

"Oh."

"And Sandhouse."

"Yes."

"About this morning. Things aren't always quite how they look."

"That right? How did they look this morning?"

"Well, I mean . . . oh, you know. The way things were, you would think . . ."

"What would I think?"

"Oh, dammit, Sandhouse. Don't be thick. You know perfectly well what I mean."

"Haven't the least godammed idea."

"Well, what I mean is that . . ."

"Petersen."

"Yes?"

"There are some people in the world who are big enough minded that they don't have to be thinking all the time. And one of the times that they 'specially don't have to be thinking is when something that isn't their business happens to be what there is around to think about. I'm one of those guys, and it's a sure thing that if I can't be bothered to think about something, I'm not going to go to the trouble of talking about it. Not here, or in Williams Lake either."

"I see. Still, I wouldn't want you to think . . ."

"Petersen, you dumb bastard, forget it."

Whether Petersen forgot it or not, he dropped it. Although Gyp had some indifferent curiosity as to whether or not there was now or ever had been since the uncovering of Little Boy's innocence any charge that could properly be laid against him, he did not inquire, because it would have been foolish to trouble Petersen with questions about what might be the real reasons for the change in his position.

Men should not do that kind of thing to each other, any more than they should think about things, when the only thing to think about that happens to be around, happens also not to be your business—and so Gyp went on to the next thing: "You need someone to go to the phone to send for your Beaver?"

"Why, yes. Yes, I guess I do."

And so Gyp left to ride with the message that would bring the means of Petersen's leaving, and he thought, as he did so, that Petersen had suddenly become oddly silent and thoughtful. He'd seemed almost in a dream as he'd fished about in his briefcase for pencil and paper on which to write the telephone number. It was so totally unlike the crisp and businesslike way in which he seemed, usually, to do even the most incidental things.

But that was again not Gyp's business, and so he did not dwell on it. But even if he had, he would never have guessed what it was that had taken hold of Petersen, that even now Petersen pondered on, by himself back in the cabin, standing by the window, looking dreamily out.

Petersen was wondering if there wasn't some way he could get his wife to give him a bath, without it seeming as though he'd had an inadmissible change of mind about the proprieties of how he had hitherto directed their lovemaking.

XL

Daylight had for some hours been streaming through the window into the cabin, and Annie lay cosily in the warmth from Gyp's body, amused that he had slept through the breaking of the new day.

Her hand was on her own flat tummy, far down near where the seed would be, and she wondered if already the magic of new life might not be happening inside her. It might be, even in just this first time after Gyp had, without a word of explanation, given up the prevention of it.

Annie thought, a little wryly, that if it had managed to happen that time three years ago, Gyp would have had to come to grips with his irresponsibility an awful lot sooner.

But she was glad it hadn't, for she wanted the new lives that they would start, deep inside her, to be by his choice as well as hers.

He came awake then, too. She could tell it from his breathing, and she knew he would be aware more of the rain that was falling than of the daylight. It was a soft sound, the sound of the rain, but it was time to hay, and rain was bad luck.

He said: "Damned rain."

She took his hand and put it with hers over where she hoped that already they had begun a child.

It must have made him think of what he had done, of the responsibility he had accepted.

He asked: "Do you want to get married?"

"You mean the piece of paper from the government and the talk in front of the priest?"

"Yeh."

"No."

"Oh."

"I'll tell you why. That's like asking for permission to make love, and I won't do that. I married you the only way it matters a long time back. There's nothing else I have to do. It's right, the way it is."

"I see."

"Is that right for you too?"

"Yes."

"I'll tell you how stupid that government is. That government's got a law in that Indian Act that says if I marry you what they call legal, my kids won't be Indians. But if I marry you my way, what they call common law, my kids will go on the list with the tribe. Isn't that stupid?"

But whether Gyp thought that was stupid or not, she never knew, for he began to laugh in that silly way of his, and when she finally got it out of him what was so funny, it really wasn't much at all.

"Hey, that's great. Do you know what that means? That means your old man gets Upper Meadow back in the reserve. All our kids belong to his tribe, and who else gets the meadow but our kids?"

"He'll like that."

"Tell me some more about that stupid law. Can I join the tribe?"

"No."

"Damned shame."

"My dad would like it. But you can give him our kids."

"And Upper Meadow."

"And Upper Meadow."

And Annie, looking at him in the morning light, thought how odd it was that a man of such irregular features could, in the result, be so fine-looking.

She reached with her hand to make that delicate touch with the stroking of her fingertips that would excite him anew and drive him to ecstasy.

She wanted, at once, to make sure of the new life they were starting.

The new life inside her, deep inside her, where their seed lay.